RIGHT BEHIND

RIGHT

A PARODY OF LAST DAYS GOOFINESS

BEHIND

MR. SOCK

NATHAN D. WILSON

UPTURNED TABLE PARODY SERIES
CANON PRESS • MOSCOW, IDAHO

Nathan D. Wilson, *Right Behind: A Parody of Last Days Goofiness*

© 2001 by Nathan D. Wilson

Published by Canon Press
P.O. Box 8729, Moscow, ID 83843
800–488–2034 / www.canonpress.org

05 04 03 02 01   9 8 7 6 5 4 3 2 1

Cover mimicry by Paige Atwood Design, Moscow, ID
Cover Image: The Walnut of Doom

Scripture quotations in this publication are taken from the
Holy Bible: King James Version.

ISBN: 1-885767-87-0

To my wife,
who loves me
anyway

Table of Contents

ONE:
BUFORD'S FATEFUL FLIGHT

BUFORD Tin's hands were on a woman he had frequently touched. His very masculine 747 cruised on autopilot over the Indian Ocean en route to a 6 A.M. or so landing in Mauritius. Buford held his breath and refused to think of his family.

The reason why he wasn't thinking about his family is because of where his hands were. They were playing up and down Haddie Dylan's spine. The reason why they were playing up and down Haddie Dylan's spine is because of the ache that she had. It started high, but once Buford's hands were on her back it always seemed to be moving lower.

Buford was lusting. Nothing inappropriate, it was normal for his age. But even so, he probably should have been passing out peanuts and napkins and thinking about his wife back in Chicago. He kept rubbing.

Buford's wife Eileen was attractive, and even vivacious upon occasion. She was forty, and even that was OK with Buford. But she had recently gotten caught up in an obsession. She had started going to church on a regular basis and could only talk about God.

God was OK with Buford Tin. Buford even enjoyed church occasionally, as long as there were plenty of skits. But Eileen had recently hooked up with a smaller congregation where the skits were more pointed. Everybody on stage always seemed to be looking at him as if to say, "This skit's for you, Buford. Listen up!" And he was more than a little uncomfortable with that. Sometimes people would even come up to him afterward and say things like, "How'd you like the skit?"

"It blessed my socks off!" had become his standard response. But these days he found more ways to be busy on Sundays. He joined a Sunday morning Chess Club, a Step Aerobics class, and had even enrolled in a Community Betterment program called "Knick knacks 'n' You: A step by step guide to creating your own knick knacks." It covered all the bases. He bought woodcarving tools and some pastel acrylic paint, and he had created a whole assortment of wooden shepherds and children. He had even made a goat.

The Haddie Dylan in Buford's backrub spell was actually Buford's boss. She was the senior flight attendant and had a stellar aviation career in her past.

So, when she said her back ached, Buford rubbed. He said that it was his duty as a flight attendant and joked that he would do it for anyone on the flight, but when talking with himself, he always chalked his actions up to his own libido. It's true that Haddie was rather attractive, but if Buford's wife Eileen hadn't been too wrapped up in her Bible studies for love, Buford wouldn't have given Haddie a second glance. He was a very tame puppy when tended.

Buford was no prude, but he was a coward. He very much wanted to be unfaithful to his wife Eileen, and he very much wanted that unfaithfulness to find its fruition in his boss Haddie Dylan. But he did not initiate any infidelity. He never had. He usually made out with girls at Christmas parties, but he always felt guilty afterward. But his wife never suspected any-thing—not from *her* flight attendant. Buford was known for his upright and stalwart behavior. He was the man who once consumed three eggnogs during a snowy Christmas delay at O'Hare and then had voluntarily grounded himself, because he feared that his ability to walk the aisle may have been impaired. He had even volunteered to pay for the replacement that Tri-Con had to call in. Instead, his airline had made him a poster-boy for self discipline in wise flight attending.

"We'd better pass out some more pillows," Haddie said. Buford was sad to end the rub, but he knew she was right. He let go of her supple back and gave her one last squeeze on the neck.

"Ow," she said.

"Sorry," he said, and they headed off. Buford went to check the pilots first. When he opened the cockpit door, he was greeted by the teething palette of pastels that composed the reluctant sunrise.

"Hey Bufe!" the pilot, whose name was Steve, said. "Glad you could join us."

"That was a fragment," Buford said. "This is an intellectual story. Please speak in complete sentences."

"Roger that, Buford. Sorry. I am glad you could join us for such a lovely sunrise. The sun looks like it's going to be a big, orange, burning ball."

"Wow!" Buford said. "It really does. Do either of you guys want anything? A pillow or a drink?"

"I am fine thanks, over," said Phil the copilot.

"Roger. I, too, am fine, Buford, over," said Steve the pilot.

"Great!" Buford said. He turned and walked back into the big, tube part of the airplane. It was in the big tube part that a surprise awaited him.

Next to a window in business class, a writer huddled over his laptop. It was one of those new neat ones, that looked like a smashed gumdrop. Suddenly, he shut his high-powered machine, swearing by his dead mother's memory to return to his journal later. At thirty, Buff Williamson was the youngest ever nearly-senior writer for the world famous magazine *Globe of*

Weekly Doom. He was envied by everyone at the magazine for his amazing acumen in typing quickly and also for his Pulitzer Prize, which he had earned in sixth grade for a paper entitled "The Baking-Soda Volcano and Me." It had revolutionized the world of papier-mâché science fair projects. After being catapulted into instant stardom, he paid his own way through an elite high school for upstarts by ghostwriting bad apocalyptic fiction. Luckily, at that early age he had no aesthetic depth, so his writing was tailor— made for the profession. His first series went big and he was able to afford an Ivy League education (a phrase that will be frequently dropped in this story so as to achieve that intellectual feel that we all so desperately strive for). While at Princeton, (Princeton is in the Ivy League) he kept the source of his money a secret out of embarrassment, a wise move, but he progressed well. Upon graduation he went straight to the *Globe of Weekly Doom*, where he made a pile of money and frequently wrote cover stories. A cover story is a good thing to frequently write. Buff's success was no surprise to his bosses; it was right in keeping with his Ivy League record. The reason Buff's family isn't mentioned is because his mother was dead, and he didn't get along with his father Glen, or his brother Geoffrey. We don't really have time to go into it now; all that's important is that his family was quite blue collar and resented Buff's Ivy League experience. Ivy League experiences are frequently resented.

Buff's real name was Cameroon. That is what all

of his Ivy League acquaintances knew him by. But once he had made it nationally with *Weekly Doom*, he had needed a nickname. It had puzzled the office for a while, as all his coworkers struggled to come up with one. He had recommended Buck because he said that he was always bucking tradition, authority, convention, social stigmas, taboos, and not least of all, poaching laws. But everyone thought Buck was as stupid as something we can't say in this book. Who had ever heard of calling someone Buck because of their particular philosophy of authority and convention? The next suggestion had been Pudge. That had been rejected because of the arrival of another employee even more suited to the name than Buff. Buff had been settled upon eventually and had stuck like sticky stuff.

Buff didn't mind the name—it sounded hip and relevant to any who might eventually read an endtimes story about him. It was just the sort of name that would catch the attention of those whose attention needed to be caught. It sounded large. He didn't care as much for the *reason* behind his nickname. A year or so-ish into Buff's time at *Weekly Doom* he called in sick. No one believed that the call was genuine, and, as it was a slow day at the office, a group of Buff's envious coworkers who did not share Buff's Ivy League experience (including Pudge) went around to Buff's apartment. He was sick, so sick that he didn't notice that they had come into his apartment. And so it was that the office of *Globe of Weekly*

Doom discovered that young Cameroon not only slept in, but also hung out in, the buff. Buff had been his name ere since. But now, lest we completely lose track of our story, let us temporarily rejoin Buff by his window in business class before we begin further reminiscences crucial to the believable, apocalyptic development of our story.

Buff sat by his window in business class and watched the sun come up like a single tooth in a bleeding gum. He remembered that time in Israel. You know, that time when he became a deist and began to think that he led a charmed life because he was always, to coin a phrase, in the right place at the right time.

Four hundred and twenty-two days earlier, his May 1 cover story (May 1 is the Russian New Year) had placed him in Israel to interview Heinz Rosenbeet, the Nobel prize winner in chemistry. Rosenbeet had walked away with the prize after his spectacular achievement in Israel. He had unlocked the genetic mystery behind zucchini production. Israel's desert sands now bloomed with the plants, and Israel had found a prosperity that they hadn't seen in a decent amount of time, say about twenty-five years. Maybe more. They had at least matched the zucchini production of that runaway squash patch back behind the house.

Israel's Arab neighbors finally realized what a worthless piece of real estate the country was and made peace. But not everyone was cheerful with the

Holy Land. Russia, Albania, and several aboriginal
clans of New Zealand harbored a deep grudge—no
one quite knows why—and they launched a surprise
attack on Israel. They sent tens of thousands of planes
(some of them twice to meet the necessary numbers),
several missiles, ten dirigibles, and thirty-two canoes
in a missing-man formation. Everyone was surprised.
There was no real objective or purpose to the attack
other than the innate depravity of Russians. It was
complete mindless villainy the likes of which could
only be found in Buff's ghostwriting. They simply
wanted Israel gone from the face of the place. To say
that the Israelis were caught off guard, by what Buff
Williamson had written in his cover story piece, was
fairly comparable to the statement that has, at times,
been made regarding oceans and wetness, or saltiness,
or anything along those lines that oceans are well-
known for. But that was only the first of the surprises.

Buff had been out in the patch with Heinz when
the first wave arrived. Sirens screamed, and everyone
ran as fast as their little legs could carry them for
cover. As Buff ducked into a handy military bunker
with Heinz, he glanced over his shoulder at the devas-
tation. But something was strange. There were the
New Zealand fighter-bombers; there were the Russian
canoes; there were the nuclear warheads. He could see
them all. But there was something else going on. Buff
turned and walked back outside. At least outside he
would see what killed him.

Israeli radar had been as surprised as anyone else

when the attack came, but now that it was on top of things again, it clearly discerned Albania's insignia on the warheads. It was then that the Israelis knew that they were looking death in the face. Albania never parleys. But the radar spoke up; there was something else going on. Explosions roared all around. It sounded like there were probably some flames involved. But there were much bigger things than planes and missiles in the air. Only Buff and Israeli radar actually saw what happened.

Large parts of the sky were falling. Huge, jagged pieces of blue were falling to the Hebrew soil, and with them, they brought the enemy. Fireballs and nuclear warmth reached the ground as the sky itself reared its head to defend God's people from previous dispensation. Wherever Buff saw an explosion, a split second later he saw a splinter of sky come barreling out of the smoke. Every plane in the sky ran into falling pieces of the sky. Every missile was detonated way up, up, high, so high that no one could get hurt. Every canoe was splashed between blues. But perhaps the most remarkable aspect of the incident was the casualty count. Nobody got hurt.

The sky crushed the missiles and planes and separated them from all of their nebulous, unknown, and terribly useful combustible materials. The metal wreckage of the crafts all tumbled into dumpsters outside needy recycling centers and art galleries specializing in welding. The combustible materials that made them go zoom all landed outside power plants.

Israel's vast natural resources could go untouched for, oh, I don't know. . . six years? Is that right? Anyway, nobody got hurt. Afterward, the bodies that fell out of the planes when the sky hit them were piled in a mound in an attempt to attract vultures and fulfill prophecy. Eventually the Israelis gave up and just burned them.

Buff became a deist that day. His morning devotional was Ezekiel 38 and 39.

And the first chapter still hasn't ended. The Rapture is coming.

We now jump back to Buff where we left him so long ago, gazing out a window at a poorly described sunrise.

An old woman sat across the aisle from him, a passed out drunk next to him. He turned from his window and looked at the old woman. She had a pair of cotton nylon blend underpants in one hand and dentures in the other. She stared at Buff in shock.

"Excuse me mister," she said.

"Yes?" Buff said.

"My Harold," she said.

"Yes?" Buff said.

"He's gone. He's just gone, vanished, disappeared. Could you help me find him?"

"I'm afraid that there is going to be no finding him, Ma'am."

"Why?"

"Has he left all material things behind him? Clothes, dentures, hairpiece?"

"Yes."

"Then he has finally turned his back on this world of matter and all things evil. He has jumped right out of the corruption that matter entails. He has taken everything essential to his being and left the rest behind. He has reached the enlightened world of forms where there is no jewelry but spiritual jewels, where dentures cannot go, where everyone is naked. He has been Raptured."

"How do you know?" the woman said.

"I write bad apocalyptic fiction. I know things. Endtimes are my game."

"What is that?" the woman said.

"What?" Buff said.

"That pink thing in Harold's seat. Right there in his trousers. It's wet." Buff looked closely, and was surprised.

"Ma'am, I'm afraid that's Harold's appendix. It's been left behind."

"Oh, how terrible!" Ma'am said, and she cried herself to sleep.

We left Buford surprised in the big tube part of the airplane. We join him again now. He walked out of the cockpit in time to suddenly see a woman walking toward him, but more importantly, toward the lav, which is what people in the know call airline restrooms. She had the kind of look that attracts TV

Baptists. Her hair was big, bleached, and beautiful. Her face was very tastefully painted, and her outfit was a very classy evening dress. Buford smiled. For a split second he thought neither of Haddie nor his wife. His mind and eyes were only on this Baptist beauty as she walked toward him in slow motion. Suddenly she was gone. Her dress was empty and it slid down onto the floor under a pile of blonde wig. Buford stopped. He was surprised. The people on either side of the aisle were surprised, at least those who were still there. Some of them had disappeared as well.

Haddie had been impatiently stuck behind a blonde walking in slow motion. She was simply trying to pass out pillows, and this woman insisted on walking down the aisle in frame-by-frame. She was relieved when the blonde fell into a pile of clothes on the floor. There stood Buford on the other side. His mouth hung open.

"Hello, Buford," Haddie said.

"Only one request for a pillow. Do the pilots need anything?" She turned to Buff who sat on her right or left. Anyway, he was to one of her sides. "Here's your pillow," she said.

"Thanks," Buff said. "Have you noticed that some people are being Raptured?"

"Raptured?" Haddie said. "I've never heard that word."

"I have," Buford said. "I used to do beach evangelism over Spring Breaks in Daytona with Campus

Crusade. I spent most of my time talking about the endtimes, and especially the Rapture. So this is it?"

"It couldn't be anything else," Buff said. "Look at the stuff left behind. It is made up entirely of things nonessential to being. Even appendixes are being left behind."

Haddie bent and picked up the blonde wig at her feet. Beneath it was a small pile of fillings, one crown, two contact lenses, a greasy smudge of makeup, two breast implants, and one appendix.

"Whoa," Haddie said. "You leave everything behind?"

"Yes," both Buff and Buford said.

"Even implants?"

"Especially implants," Buff said. "You see Haddie, in Heaven all women are flat-chested. Holiness has to be maintained."

"Yeah, I guess it does," Haddie said. "Are you guys gonna convert?"

"I'm too intellectual and scientific to convert right away," Buford said. "I work in the aviation industry and will not acknowledge God or Christianity until my analytic mind has been satisfied. How about you, Buff?"

"I went to the Ivy League," Buff said.

"So your intellect also needs satisfaction before converting?" Haddie said.

"I am also a Pulitzer prizewinner. Thought and proof always come before action in my life. Right now, my logical mind is wondering if I really want to serve a God that won't allow implants. Also, in my rational, Ivy League-trained fashion, I am wondering if we will be able to land in Mauritius, as it is notoriously Evangelical, and there probably aren't enough baggage handlers."

"I will go talk to the pilot," Buford said. And he turned and headed back to the cockpit.

"Buff? That is your name isn't it?" Haddie said.

"Yes. It's a nickname," Buff said.

"Why are you called Buff?"

"Because of my mental stature."

"I thought it was probably because you slept naked. Anyway, if this is the Rapture, isn't Satan or something supposed to show up and make things horrible?"

"Actually," Buff said, "The Antichrist shows up first. Later on comes the Beast and then eventually Christ comes back. The first seven years after the Rapture is called the Tribulation, but all that will be in later books. This one doesn't really go anywhere. It just dabbles in the puddle of the Rapture itself and its aftermath. Why? Does the sheer terror of the Tribulation and the Antichrist inspire your intellectual mind trained in the aviation industry with a desire for conversion and acceptance in Heaven?"

"No. I was just thinking that if there really is an Antichrist or someone who will rule the world, I would like to track him down and bear his child," Haddie said.

"Wow," Buff said. "That's quite a goal. Just

remember to believe in yourself and all your dreams will come true. If I happen to meet the Antichrist in my journalistic capacities, I wouldn't mind pimping you."

"Really? You really are so terrific and intellectually trained. Would you really do that for me?" Haddie said.

"Sure. Antichrists get lonely too."

"Are you sure?" Steve the pilot asked.

"Yes, I'm sure. The Rapture has happened. We are missing people. Not that it's a huge deal, but it might mean flying back to Chicago. Mauritius might be understaffed," Buford said.

"I think Buford's right," Phil the copilot said. "We don't know what kind of chaos would await us in Mauritius, over."

"How can we fly back to Chicago from the Indian Ocean? We're almost there guys, over," Steve the pilot said.

"You don't understand," Buford said. "We belong to bad Christian fiction. We can be in Chicago as soon as we want to be. I'll get a bag and collect the leftovers. Will you make an announcement to let everybody know what happened?"

"Sure I will, over," said Steve the pilot.

Buford was already walking the aisle when the announcement came.

"Folks," came Steve the pilot's P/A voice, "we'd

like to thank you first of all for choosing Tri-Con Air for all your travel needs. We appreciate your business. As you may have noticed, a fairly significant number of our passengers have disappeared. There is nothing to be worried about. A flight attendant is currently gathering the left-behind appendixes so as to prevent any health hazard. As for the remainder, if a relative of yours has disappeared, then their leftovers are obviously yours. Otherwise, feel free to help yourselves to anything left by anyone in your row. For those of you unfamiliar with dispensational eschatology, this is the Rapture. Those of our passengers who were Christians just got sucked into Heaven. We have contacted Mauritius ground control and discovered that they don't have any airport employees left behind, so we will be returning to Chicago. Estimated time of arrival will be 6:45 A.M. Thanks again for choosing Tri-Con Air."

While Buford was collecting the appendixes, he began to discover some interesting aspects of the Rapture. First, the very fact that the appendixes were left behind was curious. But then he began to discover that other things had been left behind and some others taken, things he would not have expected. Second, he encountered a woman who, placing her son's appendix in the garbage bag, expressed concern that she was unable to find her son's underpants or socks. She did have the tag to his underwear, but the underwear itself had been taken. This theme was repeated with T-shirts, and sweatshirts as well. In fact, very quickly,

Buford began to suspect something. He stopped about two-thirds of the way back in the plane and looked down his pants. Sure enough, his own underwear was gone; only the tag and the elastic remained. Everything 100% cotton had been taken. His feet were bare inside his shoes. He looked around the plane. There were many shirtless people, even pantless, depending on the brand. People everywhere were putting on the clothes that had been worn by the Christians. It was very easy to tell which khakis really were cotton through and through and which were a cotton-hypocrisy blend.

"Lucky that our airline outfits are polyester," thought Buford, and he continued picking up appendixes, moles, and the occasional tumor. Haddie was collecting from the other direction. Suddenly, Buford had a thought.

"Haddie!" Buford yelled. "My wife was a Christian."

"Yeah, so?" Haddie said.

"She just got Raptured," Buford said.

"So?" Haddie said.

"I'm available!" Buford said. "You know, for a physical relationship."

"Buford," Haddie said. "That would have been fine with me while your wife was alive. But I've got far bigger opportunities than that now. Buff Williamson is going to introduce me to the Antichrist, and I'm going to have his child. C'mon Buford! Just think of all the opportunities. The world is restructuring—no more cotton or Christians. Think of all the possibilities there are for those of us lucky enough to be left behind."

"I don't know, Haddie," Buford said. "I'm beginning to feel like an appendix."

TWO:
THE PRETRIB PREFUNC

BUFORD Tin stood ashen-faced in the cockpit. Half an hour from touchdown in Chicago, everyone on the plane knew that the Rapture had happened. This was fairly exciting news because of the social ramifications. Housing would be a lot cheaper. Making out in the park would be less offensive to the general public. The easily offended had all been Raptured. But there were other issues as well. All of the children on the plane had been taken. He wondered if that were true of all the children in the world. If it were, he would certainly miss all the sounds of the happy children of Chicago playing in the streets. Haddie had been right: the removal of all Christian and cotton influence on the world certainly presented some amazing opportunities. But the simultaneous disappearance of millions all over the globe had still resulted in chaos beyond imagination.

Buford Tin had been quite forthright in his explanations to passengers. He had told them all he knew about dispensational eschatology. He had described the beast, its mark, and all the antics of the Antichrist as best he could. He had delved into the books of Daniel, Revelation, Numbers, Isaiah, Ezekiel, and several portions of the Apocrypha. All in all, he had passengers fairly well prepared for what was coming. He commended all of them on their wisdom in waving off all evangelistic efforts up to this point, as it was obvious that, according to dispensational theology, the Christians missed out on all of the fun. Apocalyptic fiction makes it clear that being left behind is where all the action is. He had encouraged them not to convert to Christianity until their intellect had been satisfied and all of their emotional needs had been met. He had then gone into the cockpit to watch the landing. This was pretty irregular, but when people disappear, a few rules have to go.

Flights from all over the country were being rerouted to Chicago, and it wasn't for any Cubs game. As the plane settled into a holding pattern for O'Hare, the full Rapture impact began to come into view. Visibility was good despite the towering pillars of smoke that completely enshrouded the runway. Only two runways were open, and they were being used as a parking lot for jets. Landing would be hard for Steve the pilot, but Buford was there to encourage him. Everyone on board was looking death in the eye, which explains why Buford's face was ashen at the beginning of this chapter.

They landed safely but unfortunately were told
that they were going to have to walk to the terminal
after jumping out of the plane onto one of those
jumbo, inflated yellow slides.

"Jump down that?" the old woman who had lost
her Harold said to Buford. "I can't jump down that.
I'm old."

"Fine. Stay then," Buford had said. As you might
have noticed, Buford was getting testy. All the passengers who were able jumped down the slide followed
by the flight crew. The rest were left behind.

It looked like a Wal Mart on Christmas Eve. It
was as if everywhere Buford and Haddie looked there
were haggard people looking for Beanie Babies.

A golf cart had gone by and offered Buford and
Haddie a ride, but Buff was left to fend for himself.
When he got to the terminal, he went straight to the
Tri-Con Club, for members only. When he arrived, he
encountered resistance.

"Hello," Buff had said to the lady at the desk.

"Hello," she said, and he tried to walk by her.
"Just hold it right there, buster. Are you a member?
You don't look like a member." Buff had responded
with a laugh that only Ivy League men use.

"Not a member?" Buff said. "Is the pope a
member?" And he produced his membership card,
which showed that he was the number one passenger
in the world. Whenever Buff Williamson showed up
for a flight, he had to be allowed to ride in the cockpit. He must also be immediately provided with a

handmade Amish pretzel at no extra charge.

"Buff Williamson?" the lady at the desk had said. "You are a legend around here. The reason I know who you are is because I studied papier-mâché in college. Your Pulitzer prizewinning paper completely overhauled my thoughts on piñatas. You were at Princeton weren't you?"

"Yes," Buff said. "It's in the Ivy League."

"I know," the lady said.

"Good, Buff said."

"How tall are you?" the lady said.

"Tall, Buff said."

"Do you always say, 'Buff said,' after all of your dialogue?" the lady said.

"You obviously are unfamiliar with apocalyptic literature," Buff said.

"I am," the lady said. "Why does that matter?"

"Because there are only two options in apocalyptic literature," Buff said. "The first is as follows: When writing dialogue, at the end or the middle of every line the author must insert the phrase 'he said,' 'she said,' or someone's name followed by the word 'said.' Of course, real authors who don't write apocalyptic fiction prefer the word 'said' to all the many creative options that an amateur will come up with. But they will lace it through their dialogue, not distracting from what is being said by saying 'said,' but using it so the reader can keep track of the speaker. Only the good apocalyptic writer, or an eighth grader writing for an assignment, will give you the 'said' phrase following every speech. But there is also the other option. The second option is to leave the speaker completely unnamed. This is useful because it is hip and keeps the reader interested, because he is always trying to discern the speaker. It goes something like this:

'Why?'

'What?'

'Where have you been?'

'Nowhere in particular. How is the Rapture treating you?'

'Well, the traffic is rough.'

'Is your mother still a masseuse?'

'Sure, you need a rubdown?'

'Are you ready for a physical relationship?'

'No.'

"In this way the reader is forced to go back and count lines in order to discover the speaker. But all this is inappropriate at a time like this. Let me into the club before I do something surprising," Buff said. And he entered.

Upon entering the club he immediately began hacking open his expensive laptop in an attempt to hook it up to the phone and run a continuous dialing program and jam up the lines. But we have spent too much time on Buff already and spent it ill. We must move on to other snippets of insignificant Rapture moments.

Bufe Jr. hadn't been at the youth "lock-in" long when weird things began to happen. His mom had kissed him good-bye and embarrassed him in front of his friends. He had then run inside and quickly found the girl he wanted to be caught in a corner with later that night. He decided on Amber. She was a year older than he and far more pubescent. He had sidled up and exchanged pleasantries, inviting her to watch him play ping-pong. He had been practicing in the basement at home. She had agreed but made it clear that she would only watch him until one of the youth pastors showed up. Then she would have to go flirt with him until backrubs were exchanged. It was proving to be a pretty standard lock-in. He wondered who would streak tonight.

The youth group at Hoping to Endtimes Bible Church had always been impressive. They had a large outreach, a solid core group, and relatively few pregnancies. This was their big outreach for the school year. They had advertised at all the local high schools for a night of free pizza and a movie. They had ordered fifty pizzas and rented a big screen to show the *Left Behind* movie. The film had been picked because of its power and acting. But the film was never shown.

Bufie was beating a bigger boy at ping-pong with Amber watching when he was jerked out of his clothes. It was as if he had been grabbed by the back of the neck and yanked ten feet off the ground. His jeans, shirt, shoes, and hat were left on the ground.

He was left hanging above the ground in nothing but a pair of tighty-whities that were missing their waist band and tag. He was surprised. Looking around him he discovered that other people were suspended too. About one-third of the kids were hanging in the air; the rest were on the ground with mouths agape. The sanctuary that was being used for the lock-in was large, but it was still full of kids. Some of them were quietly sitting in the air in varying degrees of undress, some of them were quietly standing down on the floor eating pizza and gazing at their now nude, or nearly nude friends. Suddenly, Buford Jr. began to laugh.

"Ha, Ha, Ha!" he laughed. "It's the Rapture! Ha! I don't care if you see my butt, 'cause it's the Rapture, and I'm going, and you all are getting left behind! I'm going to Heaven Tom, and you have to start ninth grade!"

"Where are your braces?" Amber said.

"Where I am going I don't need them. They are like you. . . left behind!" Buford said. Amber started crying and bent over to look at the pile of stuff little Buford was leaving behind. There was the tangle of wire that had been bracing his teeth, and there was something else, something pink and wet. Amber picked it up and held it so Buford could see it. He was still about ten feet up, as were another seventy kids.

"What's this?" she said. Bufie looked down closely and opened his mouth to answer. Then, suddenly, he was jerked the next twenty feet to the ceiling of the sanctuary. With a resounding "thump," seventy

heads hit the wood and light fixtures. Seventy unconscious kids lay stricken on the ceiling.

"What are we going to do?" Amber said. "Should
we get them down?" She looked around the room at
the remaining sinners. "Oh, I'm glad all the youth
pastors are still here. Should we call the fire department?"

Eileen hadn't been home long when she hit the ceiling.
She was far luckier than her son. He had twenty feet
of acceleration before he hit the ceiling, and he had hit
wood. Eileen only had twelve feet to go, in her hus-
band Buford's trophy house. She had been on the
phone with the pastor's wife. They had recently
become fast friends because of mutual neglect on the
parts of their husbands.

Eileen's head had put a sizable hole in the dry-
walled ceiling of the family room, but she hadn't been
knocked out. When she gathered her wits and realized
what had happened, she looked around the ceiling
where she sat and realized that she still held the
phone.

"Susan?" she asked.

"Oh my, Eileen are you still there?" came the
reply.

"Yes dear, did you just hit your ceiling?"

"I surely did, dear. You know this must be the
Rapture," Susan said.

"Really! You think so?" Eileen said. "I always

34

thought that the Rapture would be instantaneous. Zip, Zip. Everything left behind, clothes, jewelry."

"You still have clothes on? All my rings and clothes are gone. I even think one of my organs fell out. At least there's a pink, fleshy thing on the floor with all my clothes. I wonder why I'm still fat."

Eileen looked at herself. Her wedding ring was gone, her earrings, but all her clothes were still on. She looked down at the floor. There was a small pile of jewelry and what looked like fillings, and then there was a pink, fleshy thing like Susan said. And...oh my.

"Susan, my nose job fell out!" Eileen said.

"Oh, honey, how embarrassing," came the response.

"I always tried to keep it a secret. Buford bought it for me as an anniversary present. How embarrassing, how embarrassing! I have to go back to a piggie nose now that I'm going to Heaven?"

"Well, you won't need a good nose anymore. Why would you want a sexy face in Heaven?" Susan said.

"I want to look pretty for Jesus! Oh, I don't know if I want to go anymore," Eileen sobbed. "I always thought that I would be beautiful in Heaven." She put her hands to her face and wept.

"Eileen, I'd far rather have your problem than mine. You just have a piggie nose. I'm fat, really fat. Do you think Jesus cares how we look? Physical things don't matter. They never have. I don't think there is probably such a thing as beautiful in Heaven. We will all be equal—all the same."

"Then how come you are still fat if we are all going to be equal?" Eileen asked.

"I haven't been changed yet. I have yet to receive my eternal body."

"But your appendix already fell out. Why would that leave before your fat?" Eileen asked.

"Eileen, you are starting to get a little irritating. Just because you're so skinny. . ."

"Susan, I just noticed something else," Eileen said.

"What?" Susan asked.

"My unibrow is back. I've waxed it since college and then had electrolysis treatment, but it's back, and all the collagen has fallen out of my lips. Oh, my hair is gray, all the coloring is gone!" Eileen hung up before Susan could respond. She was crying again. She leaned back on the ceiling and cried herself to sleep.

Buford was sitting in the Tri-Con flight attendant locker room. He had just showered and was watching TV while he dressed. He was going to call home to see if his family had all disappeared, but the dial-up loop on Buff's computer had jammed all the lines at the airport. So, instead of calling he was just going to catch a cab home, but all the taxis were jammed in the pileups caused by the Rapture. Traffic was miserable, what with the Rapture and all. At first Buford had thought that the Rapture would just be a jolly game. A game where he could chase Haddie because his wife was in Heaven. But now he was realizing that things like traffic would be tough because of how many minivans had been left empty, careening through traffic, when their Evangelical drivers disappeared. Luckily, their bumperstickers had warned as much.

The TV was showing the news. Or, the news was being broadcast; anyway, Buford was watching the news, little knowing that his wife was asleep on the ceiling at home, and his son was bleeding and unconscious on the ceiling of the church. Various clips of Rapture chaos were flitting across the screen. One of the things that struck Buford was the inconsistency in vanishings. In some situations people had disappeared immediately, leaving behind clothes and anything else unessential like jewelry or superfluous organs, tumors, moles, and growths. In news clips, the other vanishing people hung in the air for a few seconds, or even minutes, before they swirled their way up like they were being flushed into the sky. The newsman was also talking about the differences.

"As you can see in this home video clip, only the child who is actually celebrating his birthday remains. He is the oldest child at the party and is turning twelve. All the eleven year olds were gone in a twinkling, including the one falling out of the tree in the background. Experts have explained this particular age discriminatory phenomenon as something called the 'age of accountability.' Apparently, the eleven year olds were unaware of the consequences to their sin, while now that the birthday boy is twelve he is tried as an adult and gets to stick around for the Tribulation.

"Which brings us to our next story—Who will the Antichrist be? When will he emerge and lead our world into the Tribulation? But first this last Rapture clip just in from Australia. It is perhaps the clearest manifestation of the varying degrees of intensity that the Rapture has used.

"Watch as this rather large ten year old runs along the diving board of his grandfather's pool. His name is Algernon. While it has been fairly common for appendixes, tonsils and adenoids to be left behind, this is the first instance of anyone leaving behind hair and fat."

Buford sat, riveted as he watched a large redheaded boy in yellow trunks bound down the diving board. With his final jump he pounded off the board into the air. With his arms up he shot straight up while his hair, trunks, and belly fell and smacked onto the pool's surface.

"Watch again in slow motion," the newsman's voice said. Buford watched again.

Cleo had never much liked her family. Her dad was a flight attendant, her mom was a religious nut, and her brother was a pietistic, self-righteous little twit. Her full name was Cleopatra Lucine Tin. She was still bitter about it. She had left the house as soon as she possibly could, which had been at the age of eighteen, for college. She was terribly smart, and as she will later be an important character representing goodness, we must point out that she was at Stanford on a full ride. Which, while it isn't actually Ivy League, is at least terribly expensive and takes a huge percentage of its professors' grant money. In other words, we may all feel intellectual feelings in regard to Cleo. We haven't mentioned that Buford had a daughter yet, not because this is a poorly written book, but because we didn't want to. It would not have fit within our plan. Remember, we are in Chapter Two and we still haven't introduced the Antichrist. At least we are introducing Cleo now.

While Cleo was smart, she was still having issues with authority. She had tracked down the roughest guy she could find and attached herself to him, simply to aggravate her mother. She frequently sent home pictures of her "boyfriend's" new tattoos. He wasn't actually her boyfriend. He just let her ride on the back of his motorcycle because it made him look good. He also didn't have any tattoos. Cleo just cut pictures out of magazines and said they were pictures of her boyfriend's toe, knee, chest, neck or whatever the case currently was.

When the Rapture came, Cleo was on the back of his motorcycle in the middle of his gang on the way to a party. She felt him jerk in front of her. Her arms were around his middle and after the initial jerk she felt him slowly sliding up in her arms. He clamped his legs tighter on the bike and grabbed the handlebars with the grip of death.

39

"Don't let go," Pedro muttered to Cleo. "Hold me."

"What's happening?" Cleo asked.

"The Rapture. It's the Rapture. I was going to tell you. I was. I'm sorry Cleo," Pedro said.

"What? You can't be Raptured! Only Christians are Raptured! You're rough. You're tough! You can't be good." Cleo said.

"Oh, yes, I can," Pedro said. "But it's pretty embarrassing to get Raptured right in front of your own motorcycle gang. I think I can hold on until no one is looking."

Suddenly, with a jerk, Cleo was knocked off the back of the bike. She landed, rolled, and looked up. Pedro had hung onto his handlebars, but his legs had been torn off the bike, knocking Cleo off. Pedro was now riding down the road in the center of his gang. His feet were straight up in the air, but his hands still tight on the front of the bike. The front wheel lifted off the ground, and then Pedro was gone. His bike spun out of control. His leathers hit the asphalt. Cleo stood up.

"If this is the Rapture," she thought, "I have to get home to be with Dad, because now that everything bad is happening, I realize that I truly love him. I realize that I always have. I realize that I have just been looking for acceptance. I realize it is time that I do the accepting. I must affirm myself and then aid others. I will be a good person first, proving that I have access to righteousness all by myself; then I will

consider converting. For now my intellect needs
satisfying, and I must get to Chicago." And with that,
she was gone. Where? We can't be sure—to a bus
station or an airport or somewhere. Regardless, she
was on her way to Chicago.

———————

Buff was still sitting by his laptop watching it dial
up over and over and over, jamming O'Hare's lines,
when he finally gave up. The laptop was plugged into
a payphone and the wall. He had fought with a mime
over access to the power outlet, but he had been
bigger, so his computer cord was safe. His batteries
were in reserve. It was time for desperate measures.
He couldn't afford to have no access to his email any
longer. He let his laptop continue dialing while he
prepared an alternative method.

Using toenail clippers, he snipped his sock and
began unraveling a long thread. His socks were not
cotton. Reaching into his carry-on bag, he pulled out
two Styrofoam cups and a pair of needlenose pliers.
He didn't need the pliers, but needlenose pliers look
really neat. Swiftly connecting the ends of the string to
the backs of the cups, he set one cup mouth down on
the keyboard of his laptop. The other end he held to
the mouthpiece of the payphone. Connection. Bingo.
The people in line waiting for the phone were amazed.
But that's why some people win the Pulitzer prize and
others are amazed. That's why some write the apocalyptic fiction and others read it.

Buff glanced over his email. He had one from his boss. We will not include the full text. He was needed in New York. The world had watched the Rapture, and now it was ready for the Antichrist. And the *Globe of Weekly Doom* needed Buff to find him.

———————

Buford had finished watching the news and had then chartered a helicopter to bypass the traffic and drop him off on the roof of his garage. He was halfway there.

———————

Buford Jr. had come to sprawled on the ceiling of the Hoping to Endtimes Bible Church with a youth pastor on a tall ladder pulling on his leg. The fire department had been called, but they couldn't get anywhere in the traffic, what with the Rapture and all. The youth pastors were attempting the Rapture rescues themselves.

———————

Eileen woke up because she had had a long and emotionally trying dream in which she was not allowed to look beautiful in Heaven. Not that she was ever truly beautiful on earth, but her concept of beauty ran as deep as an Evangelical's can. She never really understood what a true pursuit of beauty would mean, but she thought she did. And she tried hard in her own shallow way. Now, she had reached a conclusion. Despite the chance that she might not be allowed to wax her eyebrow in Heaven, she must go anyway. She got to her knees on the ceiling and crawled down the wall to a window. It wouldn't open. In a last reaction against the evils of the material world, she kicked the glass and crawled out into the sky.

———————

Buford Jr. screamed and leapt to his feet. The youth leader had grabbed his ankle and was trying to pull him down. "You can't keep me here!" Bufie said. "You can't! You can't! I won't stay. I'm sick of the meetings and stupid Bible studies. I'm sick of the popcorn and outreaches!" And all the while he ran. He ran past the other kids stuck on the ceiling. He jumped beams and dodged lights and reached the stained glass behind the cross. His lacking-elastic skivvies sagged and drifted to the ceiling as he hit the glass and was sucked into the sky. People were surprised. Bufie had always been the quiet type, a good kid. Slowly, the other kids on the ceiling said their good-byes to those on the floor and followed Bufie. The youth pastors wept. Their lock-in was ruined. Now nobody would stay the whole twenty-four hours.

THREE:
OF ANTICHRISTS AND THINGS

THE Antichrist of this story was born Randy Jarvis in
Tulsa, Oklahoma. His family moved shortly after his
birth to the lengthy state of Kansas. They farmed.
Young Randy had always been set aside for the
ministry. He was weak and pompous and often got
out of his chores on the plea that he was allergic to
corn and wheat. Randy fit perfectly into the misguided
mold for American pastors. He prayed passionately,
was handsy with the girls, and often volunteered to
baby-sit. After his voice broke, he began leading the
singing at his church.

Randy had always had the gift of leadership. He
led missions to Mexico and was able to keep the
tequila drinking at a minimum. He organized canned
food drives and Christmas programs. He was well
liked, and on the surface he seemed to be quite happy
with his calling in life.

Randy Jarvis grew up and became Pastor Jarvis.
He studied at a well-known dispensational seminary
and became an expert in prophecy and endtimes. His
sermons were powerful, and his church grew and grew
and grew.

Pastor Jarvis then went on to found a school. The
Endtimes Bible College of South Topeka came into
existence with Pastor Jarvis at the helm. But all was
not well inside Pastor Jarvis's head. While the school
thrived on his leadership and produced some of the
top endtimes minds in the country, the truly top mind
began to slip.

Pastor Jarvis disliked God. He knew that God was
there. He never would have entertained the idea of
atheism, but he just didn't like the God that he
preached. So, he had decided to fight Him. He knew
that in the end he would lose and go to Hell, but he
didn't care. He was a blasphemer and hypocrite and
resolved to do as much damage to the modern Church
as he possibly could.

For a short while Pastor Jarvis considered starting
a cult. That seemed like fun, and he tried it briefly, but
all the types attracted by his cult, while willing to
worship him, weren't worth being worshipped by. So,
in the end, he decided to become an evil genius. They
always seemed to have fun. He moved to Brazil and
began studying spiritual density. He also lived the
Brazilian fast-track lifestyle and killed at least one of
his business partners.

Pastor Jarvis had some time for introspection in

Brazil. But this has gone on for long enough. In the end he legally changed his name to Old Nick and raised huge investments for the founding of a Christian satellite dish network. His ultimate goal was the prevention of the Rapture. You see, though he was evil, he was still a dispensationalist. His ultimate dream was to hijack the Rapture and step into the position of the Antichrist for a wild ride through the Tribulation. . . and he believed in himself.

———————————

Two days had passed since the Rapture had surprised people. Buff had made it to New York, Buford was home hoping that Cleo would show up, and Haddie was watching the news with her cat. She was watching a police clip of a van full of teens on the way to Bible camp that was hopping down the road as the teens inside crashed into the roof. Eventually, one of them managed to open a door and squirt out the side. The rest followed and then the van sat quietly. The newsman was introducing the next story about the beginnings of the Tribulation when her phone rang. Haddie tossed her cat and went to answer.

"Hello," Haddie said. There was silence.

"Hello," said a voice on the other end. It was Buff, but Haddie didn't know that.

"Hello," said Haddie.

"Haddie?" said Buff.

"Yes, who is this?"

"This is Buff Williamson, Pulitzer prizewinner with the *Weekly Doom*. I'm calling to make good on a promise."

"What's that? I don't remember any promises," Haddie said. "What are you talking about? Oh, wait! You've met the Antichrist? You've met the Antichrist!" And she started jumping up and down just like she had at that N'Sync concert.

"I'm in his hotel room now. He's a little lonely and would like some companionship. When can you be here?" Buff said.

"Where are you?" Haddie said.

"We are in Manhattan. The Comfort Inn. When can you be here?" Buff asked.

"Probably early in the next chapter. If I get there too quickly the whole schedule of events will be thrown off. I might end up converting in the first book instead of the second, and you might convert right away. Or, the plot could be so thrown out the window that neither of us convert at all. You called a little early, but I still think we should stick to the current outline of events," Haddie said.

"You're probably right. So where are we?" Buff asked.

"We have to learn how you tracked down the Antichrist and ended up in his hotel room," Haddie said.

"Right," Buff said.

When Buff had finally made it into his New York office, he was greeted by a round of applause from the other two people who had made it into work, the secretary and one other writer he didn't like.

"Frank wants you in his office now," the secretary said. Buff walked through the rows of empty desks and into his editor's office. It may be apparent to you, as we pointed out, that there were only two other people in the office, and we have now referred to three. We weren't counting Frank.

"Steve!" Frank said as Buff entered.

"I'm Buff," Buff said.

"No you are not. Oh, but that's your nickname isn't it? But I always call you Steve," Frank said.

"No you don't. You call me Buff," Buff said. "Why are you pulling this clichéd senile boss routine? You know that's not this story. We are working with an entirely different cliché," Buff said.

"And what would that be, smartbottom?" Frank said.

"Smartbottom?" Buff said. "What story do you think you are in? You are my buddy-boss! We are two of a kind! I'm your golden boy! You always give me any assignment that I want because of how highly you think of me and I of you! And your name is Steve, not mine, yours! Why Frank all of the sudden? And now that you are calling yourself Frank and acting outside of your assigned cliché, you start saying things like 'smartbottom.' You used to be on top of things!" Buff said.

"Okay Buff! Fine. Sorry, I slipped out of character. You're right, I am Steve, but Steve is my name in the original book that we're spoofing. Do you think we're allowed to have the same name in both books? Won't we get sued? Frank works better because it in no way resembles Steve, and we won't get in trouble. As for 'smartbottom,' I think you are the one who didn't read the story description. 'No profanities, obscenities or anything off-color in any way.' That's what it said, and that's what I'm doing. The list of recommended substitutes included 'smartbottom,' and so I used 'smartbottom.' I may have slipped on the senile thing, but as far as the Frank and 'smartbottom' issues are concerned, I'm sticking to my guns," Frank said.

"Hmmm," Buff said.

"Yes, smartbottom? You wanted to say something?" Frank said.

"I still think you should be Steve. They can't accuse us of having put it in our book simply because it was in their book. Your name is Steve, and we can say that it has nothing to do with their book."

"But I am Steve in this book because I'm Steve in that book," Frank said.

"Yes, I know. But they can't prove that. For all they know it's just a happy coincidence," Buff said.

"Are you sure?" Frank said.

"Absolutely," Buff said.

"Fine, then," Steve said.

"Attaboy!" Buff said. "Besides, if they want to sue us they'll have a lot more than just your name to be angry about. They will probably think that we are attacking Christianity itself when we are actually only mocking their particular muppet version of it."

"Don't you think that it's more 'scooby snack' Christianity? I mean it's too small to be filling. It's saccharine. It lacks depth, and it has the literary structure of a *Scooby Doo* episode," Steve said.

"Wow. Do you think we should leave that part in?" Buff said.

"Absolutely. That's my only good line. But we should probably get back to the story," Steve said.

"Buff, what do you have on the Antichrist? Everybody's scrambling to find him. Tell me you've got something."

"Well," Buff said, "I do, and I don't."

"More," Steve said.

"You know I never talk about my sources, but since we're such buddies, I'll tell you. I was following a confusing lead to Mauritius when the Rapture happened. Durk Lynus, an old Ivy League buddy of mine, works over there at a satellite dish factory. He has given me a few tips throughout our friendship, but he has always been a little fruity. Well, he called me last week and told me that he had something big and asked if I believed in God. I said that I might depending on his tip. He then begged me to fly to Mauritius because he was too scared to say what he had to say over the phone. I hopped on a plane that ended up in Chicago in post-Rapture chaos."

"Did he say what his tip was regarding?" Steve asked.

"He did. He said that he had some information

regarding disappearances. It seemed tame enough, and then the Rapture came. I think this was what he was talking about. He has some insight into the Rapture that enabled him to see it coming. And Frank. . ."

"Yes, Buff?"

"Durk is not a religious man."

"Hmmm."

"Also, on one leg of my trip from Chicago to New York, I was picked up by a garbage truck. The garbage man said that he had attended an endtimes school of prophecy founded by a pastor who went around the bend and became an evil genius. He says his name was Pastor Randy Jarvis. At first I couldn't track any Randy Jarvis, but then I saw online that a former dispensational pastor named Old Nick was scheduled to address the UN on the subject of the Tribulation. Apparently he has a lot of money. I looked up Old Nick on the internet and discovered that he was born Randy Jarvis. He's in New York now and will be addressing the body tomorrow after lunch. I thought I might track him down and interview him before his speech."

"I don't know about this Jarvis guy. I think you should head to Mauritius first," Steve said.

"But Steve!" Buff whined. "He speaks tomorrow. What if the Mauritius thing is nothing?"

"I don't care. Go to Mauritius," Steve said.

"Okay," Buff said. He was very submissive when it came to conflicts of this nature. He would never dream of bucking at Steve's authority or, for that matter, at tradition or convention.

Two hours later Buff was on a flight to Mauritius. He had called his friend Durk, but there wasn't any answer. He had left a "hello" on Durk's voice mail and then hopped a plane.

Thirty-thousand feet above the Atlantic, things weren't feeling right to Buff, like something had gone terribly wrong. He thought it might be because the last time he had been above an ocean, people had started disappearing. But that wasn't it. The real reason was that Buff's trip to Mauritius didn't at all fit within the structure of this story. It was out of place, frivolous, unnecessary, and would only be used as action filler. But for now Buff could only sit and feel the wrongness.

Buford had not yet given up on Cleo. He still hoped that she would come home and try to find him. He knew that she might be gone forever. Not that she would have disappeared. He knew that she was a pagan. He'd seen the pictures of her boyfriend's tattoos. He was just hoping that she would care enough about him to try to come home.

Cleo was sobbing. She looked over at the trucker who had picked her up on the side of the Interstate. The cab of the truck was big, so she wasn't that close to him. "I want my Daddy!" she sobbed to herself. "I want my Daddy!"

The trucker's mind was elsewhere. "Have you ever eaten squid?" he asked.

Buford was trying to allay the anguish. In an attempt to stop worrying about Cleo, he had gone upstairs to look through Little Bufie's stuff and smell his wife's clothing. As he climbed the stairs and approached the French doors that led to the master suite, he noticed something for the first time that was impossible to miss.

"Why did Eileen always decorate with this crap?" he said out loud. The glass of the doors had cute little flowers and animals stenciled on them. The curtains were lace of an exceeding frilliness. The pictures on all the walls were lit up when the lights dimmed, and they were all of the same effeminate little gnome lands. He knew that in the bathroom hung the metallic rendition of that ridiculous poem about footprints on the beach; and in his bedroom—Eileen's needlepoint mantras and a studio portrait of herself with fuzzy edges. He stopped on the top stair and looked around at the landing. Directly ahead of him were the doors to his own bedroom.

"Is it something in Evangelicals that makes them so ludicrous?" he asked the walls. Then his eyes caught something else. There on a little shelf by the light fixture sat several of his creations, horrible little knick knacks with sneering faces. "I'm no better. I

lived here for years and was always saying how much
I appreciated her decorating. I guess you don't have to
be an Evangelical in order to lack an aesthetic com-
pass. Of course, I am a character in an Evangelical
book. Might it be the author's aesthetic lack that rules
my own?" With that satirical commentary Buford
went back downstairs.

He thought about watching the news but knew
that it would all be the same clips and jabber about
the Rapture and the coming Tribulation. But his
curiosity had been piqued already by the varying
Rapture incidents. The story that he had heard from
the mother of one of Bufie's friends about his own
son's departure had been highly irregular. At first he
had chalked the tale up as an exaggeration caused by
shock. Buford could piece together enough of what his
wife had said about the coming Rapture to know that
being suspended ten feet above the ground wearing
nothing but the cotton parts of your skivvies before
being knocked unconscious against the ceiling was not
included. Buford sat down on the couch.

"Wouldn't God perform a little better than that?
Kids in Australia sucked out of their own fat, and kids
in Chicago stuck on the ceiling?" he muttered to
himself. Either God was a lot less capable than all the
Christians had thought, or this wasn't the Rapture. Of
course, it could also be the case that God merely had a
sense of humor and thought it would be funny to beat
His people to a pulp on their own ceilings before
catching them up. Perhaps it was a sort of Evangelical

purgation? Every Christian was divvied varying degrees of a traumatic Rapture experience in order to cleanse them of whatever sins they were committing at the time? What had Little Buford been doing?

"No," thought Big Buford. "It can't be that." It seemed that the Tribulation was more purgative than the Rapture itself. The Tribulation would certainly purge much out of many, being the last chance for conversion. Would he be one of the converted? He remembered reading a bad book about a similar situation at some point. What had the hero done? That was easy. It was a book that Eileen had given him to prompt a conversion. She'd rented the corresponding movie. It was a little odd that such a sorry excuse for a story would become his life. He finally turned on the TV. Just as he expected: something about the upcoming Antichrist. The news station was conducting a poll of possible candidates, but nobody seemed to have settled on anything. The Tribulation couldn't start quite yet.

"Daddy?" came a voice.

"Cleo!" Buford yelled and jumped to his feet. Cleo was standing in the door with her backpack on. They rushed sobbing into a mutual embrace.

"Mom? Bufie? Are they here?" Cleo asked knowingly.

"They're gone, both of them, out windows," Buford said. Cleo burst into tears again.

"Pedro's gone too," she said.

"Pedro? That's impossible. I saw the pictures. He ca. . ."

"Yes, he can have. He was keeping it from me, and none of those pictures were of Pedro's tattoos. They were from magazines." Buford was confused.

"Would you like a cookie?" Buford asked.

"Oh yes! Yes! I've needed one for days," Cleo sobbed, and they squeezed tighter then cried each other to sleep.

Buff had wasted no time contacting Durk when he arrived in Mauritius. Only he wasn't able to reach him. Instead he left another voicemail message and went to find breakfast. He took a cab from the airport to some part of the island where breakfast was available. We are unsure what exactly it is that people eat in Mauritius, but it wasn't American.

Buff had ended up at a sidewalk café and had ordered the special. We will call it a boiled tomato and egg white omelet. He had learned to love egg whites at Princeton.

When the waiter brought him his omelet, Buff asked him for a newspaper. When it came, Buff was surprised. He was surprised because above the fold on the front page was a story about Old Nick, formerly Randy Jarvis, addressing the United Nations. It said something like, "Today Old Nick, former pastor and endtimes expert, will address the United Nations." The newspaper was as unable to come up with a believable explanation of why such a man would be giving such a speech. But below the fold waited a bigger surprise.

Buff was irritated that he would be unable to interview Old Nick Jarvis before his speech. But perhaps more irritating was the news that Durk had killed himself. There it was, right in the newspaper where Buff himself would have put it, had he written the story. Durk Lynus was dead. He had shot himself in the chest with a long-barreled Winchester repeater five times.

"How tragic," said Buff. Then something struck him. Durk had long ago lost his arms in a terrible accident! How could he have shot himself?

"Of course!" Buff said to the waiter. "They wouldn't know that he didn't have arms. But he was my roommate in college. We were in the Ivy League together. We went on pizza binges together. I was close to him, close enough to help him put on his socks. Hmmm. Whoever killed him didn't realize his secret. This is beginning to look suspicious."

"How's your omelet?" the waiter asked.

"I found some yolk."

After Buff had finished his breakfast he headed off to make a phone call. He used a phone booth and placed a call to the Mauritius branch of Scotland Yard. He was calling a friend of his, a friend of Durk's as well. Back in the good old days, before Durk shot himself, the three of them used to get together to have fun times. They met at a pub. Buff knew that Scott Henshaw could and would speak accurately about Durk's death.

"Why, thank you for calling, Mr. Williamson," Scott said.

"Scott! You know you can call me Buff. We've been buddies for how long now?" Buff said.

"Sir, I will get right on it, but I'm afraid I will have to call you back."

"Scott! Talk to me! Who killed Durk Lynus?" Buff yelled, but there had already been a click on the other end. Scott had hung up on him. "What the heck!" Buff yelled to the world. "I just want some answers! Will someone give me answers?" A woman stopped outside the phone booth.

"You know the answers as well as I do, young man," she said.

"Shush!" Buff said.

"Don't shush me! You were there when the story was explained. Were you paying attention or were you just off in the corner flirting with that Cleo girl again?"

"Hush, I haven't even met Cleo yet."

"Don't hush me! Oh, and you think I'm going to believe that after what I saw you doing with her in the parking lot? Cookies! Ha!" The woman walked on. "Ha!" she said to the air in the distance. Suddenly, the phone rang.

"Hello," said Buff.

"Buff?" Scott said.

"Yeah?" said Buff.

"Meet me at the pub," Scott said.

"Which one?" said Buff.

"Lefty's Behind."

"OK," said Buff, but Scott had already hung up again.

Buff was sitting in a booth at Lefty's Behind. Scott hadn't shown yet. Buff had assumed that Scott had meant immediately when he had said, "Meet me at the pub." Well, he would know better next time. He had already drunk half of his beer and was beginning to feel the buzz. He had asked for popcorn to absorb the alcohol, but, like Scott, it hadn't come yet. Buff wasn't much of a drinker. In reality he would have been, but because of the Evangelical context of this story, he couldn't hold his liquor. Not that this was any flaw of Buff's. It's just that the authors of his story are unfamiliar with the effects of alcohol in its various forms. So, Buff had a buzz. My, oh my! Just imagine if Scott took so long that Buff had to order a second.

Luckily, Scott walked in before Buff's first beer was drained. He came directly over and sat in the booth.

"What was with that routine on the phone? Couldn't you tell that the line wasn't secure?" Scott said.

"What do I have to be afraid of?" Buff said.

"The Antichrist," Scott said.

"Why?"

"Because he's everywhere. His long tentacles run this island as well as the rest of the Indian Ocean."

"Hmmm," Buff said. He was fond of *hmmm*. "I always thought he'd be scarier than that. He only runs the Indian Ocean?"

"Baby steps, my friend, baby steps. He started small and has gotten much bigger. What does the name Randy Jarvis mean to you?"

"Former dispensational pastor, current owner of some Christian satellite dish company. Why?"

"He killed Durk."

"Why?"

"Because Durk worked for him."

"Isn't the labor union upset? I wouldn't think that even Antichrists could do that."

"They are all dead too."

"The whole union?"

"No. I made that up. They don't know about it. You see, Durk was working on something special for Antichrist Jarvis."

"Antichrist Jarvis?"

"That's what he likes to be called. You know this whole Rapture thing? Fake. Every bit of it."

"What? Say that again."

"No. You heard the first time, and this dialogue is taking up too much room. Anyway, Jarvis hired Durk to help him with the technology to fake the Rapture, and Durk was going to give it to you. Jarvis had somehow figured out how to magnetize human essences."

"How about chimps?"

"Will you stay on topic?"

"Sorry. It's just that I'm tired of pretending that I don't know where the story is going."

"What do you mean?"

"Well, you're telling me that we haven't had a real Rapture and that the Antichrist is Jarvis but that he's not even really the Antichrist, he just thinks he is, and that all the Christians aren't really in Heaven but are actually in a. . ."

"Will you shut-up? The reader doesn't know that yet! What are you tying to pull?"

"Do you think anyone is still reading? And I fall in love with Cleo, and we both convert and so does her dad, and a lot of other people, and we form the Tribulation Team. . . Oh yeah, and you get blown up in a car bomb." Buff looked up and smiled at Scott. "You might want to get that over with now."

"You've had too much to drink."

"No. It's just that this story is so contrived to fit its preachy message, and I guess I'm just irritated that I had to come to Mauritius at all instead of interviewing Jarvis, where I should have been. Plus, I already know the end of the book, and it is such a bunch of nothing, it depresses me to be a part of it!" Buff began sobbing and put his face on the table.

"You're drunk and disgusting," Scott said and he stood up.

"I've only had one beer, not even that," Buff said looking at his glass.

"You're in an Evangelical story, by Evangelicals, for Evangelicals, written in an attempt to make more Evangelicals. One beer does it for them."

"Dammit, you're right. I'm tanked."

"You probably shouldn't say that. People will be offended."

"Why?"

"It just isn't done. Besides it's in your contract. They will probably just edit it out anyway and then fine you for contract violation. Do you want to back up and try again?"

"Humph. May as well."

"Okay, I'll start. You're in an Evangelical story, by Evangelicals, for Evangelicals, written in an attempt to make more Evangelicals. One beer does it for them."

"Dammit it, you're right. I'm tanked."

"Of course there is a benefit to Evangelical writing as well, especially the apocalyptic stuff of which we are made. . . "

"What's that?"

"You could still get back to New York in time to interview Jarvis. Temporal structure is meaningless here. Click your heels. Well, I'm off to be blown up by an Antichrist car bomb. Kiss Cleo for me, when you meet her." Scott left.

"Don't worry Scott," Buff said. "I'm *right behind* you."

Suddenly there was a terrific explosion. Buff

feigned surprise. His friend was dead. Buff fell on the floor and wept for his friend while the huge fireball tore through the bar. He was always emotional in his cups.

———————

Haddie sat impatiently. She was quite annoyed with Buff. He should have revealed how he met up with the Antichrist by now. The readers should have been prepared for her introduction to the most powerful man in the world. But instead, they dawdle in Mauritius. She was pacing her living room. Snorting, she kicked her cat and then burst into tears. The cat cried itself to sleep. Haddie kept pacing.

———————

Buff was back in New York with forty-five minutes to spare before Antichrist Jarvis addressed the venerable body that called itself the United Nations. Don't ask.

As soon as he had been allowed to, Buff got on his cell phone and called his boss.

"Steve," Buff said.

"Buff," Frank said.

"Jarvis. Hotel?"

"Are you trying to be hip and intellectual sounding? —'Cause you aren't."

"Oh, don't even start," Buff said. "I need to get to Jarvis's hotel before he heads off to his speech."

"Why?"

"Just tell me where he is."

"The Comfort Inn, Manhattan. He's in room number 103 with a whirlpool tub."

––––––––––

The door to room number 103 was opened by a small man. He was distinctly pencil-necked and balding. He wore a leisure suit of blue. There was a rhinestone horseshoe pin the size of his nose on his jacket and a twinkly sort of rhinestone look in his eye.

"Lovely day, Mr. Williamson. Or should I say Buff? The sky strikes me as almost a vast expanse," said the Antichrist.

"It is a lovely day."

"Have you noticed how blue the sky is?"

"Like your suit."

"That's why I love this suit. It makes me feel as if I were in the heavens."

"Can I get right to the point?"

"Surely, Buff, you don't need to ask."

"Great. Are you the Antichrist?"

"Have a seat, Mr. Williamson. Coffee, tea, cocoa, orange juice, vodka?"

"You are the Antichrist. Kill me if you like, but I won't pretend that you're not."

"Now Buff, why would you think such a thing about me? You must have quite a pile of information that I don't."

"Where to begin. How about here? You had Durk Lynus killed after he threatened to spill the beans to me about your pseudo-Rapture technology. You killed Scott Henshaw by car bomb because he was a throwaway character introduced simply to die, but that doesn't make it any nicer. You had one of your business partners in Rio killed. You know all about the endtimes. You hate God while you believe in His existence, and you have abducted every Christian and child having first positively magnetized the spiritual density of innocence. You sold unsuspecting Christians satellite dishes that they thought would simply bring them the best of family programming, while you actually used the dishes to project your own evil ray of negatively charged spiritual density. Such a global ray sucked the Christians with varying degrees of intensity to an undisclosed location, where you will keep them in an attempt to thwart the real Rapture which was to come this May Day." Buff ended and found that he was standing on the edge of the whirlpool tub.

"My dearest Buff, you are easily excited. Surely you don't think that you can prove any of this?"

"I can."

"How?"

"You just offered me hard alcohol."

"Yes. Why? Would you like some now?"

"No."

"Then why bring it up?"

"It is my proof and your fatal slip."

"Hard alcohol?"

"You offered me vodka."

"And. . ."

"Vodka is Russian. You not only offered me a hard alcoholic drink; you offered me a hard *Russian* alcoholic drink. I suppose that now you want me to believe that you had nothing to do with Russia's assault on the Holy Land?"

"Mr. Williamson, vodka is also Swedish."

"No. It can be made in Sweden, but it is drunk by Russians and Russians only."

"And by me."

"Ha! Exactly."

"And so you conclude that I am the Antichrist? You are very clever Buff, and I must admit the truth of your accusation. I am announcing as much at the United Nations in twenty minutes."

"You mean that I don't have a scoop?"

"You have a scoop by twenty minutes. And now Mr. Williamson, I must leave you. I have a speaking engagement. Would you care to join me? I like you and would like to offer you the position of my press secretary later in the evening."

"Sure. I'll come," Buff said, trying to hide his pleasure with his own cleverness. He had pretended to think that Jarvis was the real Antichrist. The whole time he had been talking to Old Nick Jarvis, he had been thinking about the words of his friend Scott just moments before he exploded. Actually, Buff had said the words, but he was stealing Scott's lines when he did. This Jarvis fellow had faked the Rapture and wasn't really the Antichrist, though he was an evil genius who was trying to be. Buff wasn't sure why it was important whether he was the real Antichrist or a pseudo-Antichrist, as long as he could suck people off of their appendixes and out of their fat, but somehow it still encouraged and excited him, leaving him a little tingly in the toes.

———————

Buford and Cleo both woke up and went into the kitchen to share a cookie. There, on the pink formica, sat the cookie jar. In it were cookies. Eileen had made them the week before her Rapture. When Buford lifted the lid of the jar, he wept. Inside were his favorite kind of unspecific homemade cookies. On the top of each cookie Eileen had drawn hearts in chocolate. Buford reached in and pulled a cookie out of the jar. Its essence filled the room and he suddenly clutched it to his breast.

"Cookie!" he cried. "Cookie!" he wept. "Cookie!" he sobbed. "Cookie! Cookie! Cookie!" he screamed, and he fell to the linoleum kick-sobbing violently. "Cookie." He breathed. "Oh what a sweet, sweet, little wife I had. I didn't deserve her. How could I have ever looked at another woman, especially one who wants to sleep with the Antichrist? How? Why? With cookies like these! With cookies like these..." He trailed off at the end.

"Dad? Let's go watch the news or something,"

Cleo said, munching her cookie. She had not yet
learned of the power of baked goods and their essences. Her father remained huddled up on the floor
clutching his cookie. It was a while before his breath-
ing stopped sounding like a sucking chest wound.

FOUR:
HADDIE—THE WHORE OF
BABYLON

CLEO sat watching a live broadcast from the United Nations. Sure they're unusual, but that doesn't mean that they don't exist. She had already finished her cookie and sat with a blank face lit by the screen. There was chocolate in both corners of her mouth.

"I have the pleasure of introducing a great friend and humanitarian," said Secretary General Osama Bim Laddin. "He has revolutionized the world of Christian satellite dishes, and now he promises to help us revolutionize the world. Put your hands together and give a warm United Nations welcome to Old Nick Jarvis. Come on up Nick! Yeah! Give him a hand, folks!"

Cleo sat amazed. She watched the United Nations broadcast on a regular basis and she had never seen this group of stiffs get excited about anything. But they were positively fired up.

Haddie's cat had not forgiven her for kicking it, so it left Haddie to watch TV alone. The cat was also very depressed. You see, every other pet in the neighborhood had been Raptured. They hadn't even all been dogs. Kittens had been taken too, and one chinchilla. As the only adult cat on the block, the poor creature was dealing with the despair of being left behind.

Haddie was a big fan of the United Nations and pledged every year when they had their public television drives, though she rarely followed through with a donation. She was watching the U.N., but the delegates weren't being themselves. They were excited. She wondered what was going on. The Secretary General was just finishing an introduction and the delegates leapt to their feet with a roar. Their faces were aflame with hope and generic goodness. Some of them were clapping, and others jumped up and down with their fists in the air. The delegate from the United Arab Emirates had climbed onto the shoulders of Gunga Din, the delegate from India, and the two-man tower of friendship swayed, four hands clapping, representing the welcome that both Hinduism and Islam were giving the speaker. Before Haddie's very eyes, the entire United Nations divided itself into such two-man towers. Then all the friendship towers joined hands and began singing "We are the Champions," in harmony. As the song concluded, the speaker appeared. He was a small man in a leisure suit, but he was carrying something in front of him. It was a gold pocket watch. He was holding it by the end of the chain, and it was swinging slowly like a pendulum in front of his face.

"What is he doing?" Haddie asked her cat, and then her tone changed. "Oh my! He's gorgeous!" She was now looking at a tall blonde in a pinstripe suit. His teeth were perfect, his fingers graceful, and his voice rolled as smooth as rubber pills off an eraser.

"Ladies and gentlemen!" the man said. "I stand before you at the culmination of thousands of years of preparation. I have waited for this moment as long as I can remember hating God. Of course that hatred started in 1965 when as a sixteen-year-old boy I was shot with a bottle rocket. It hurt really badly and my hatred began!" The crowd erupted in cheers and tried to start singing again. He wouldn't let them. They were surprised.

"As I grew older, I only had one dream. I dreamt that I would become the most powerful man in the world and would be called Antichrist. That is all that I ever wanted, and now I have it." There were more cheers. Haddie's cat wondered what Haddie was clapping about. "I appreciate your inviting me to speak to you today, but even more I appreciate your

offer of the Secretary Generalship of these United
Nations."

Buff was sitting in the back of the...whatever it is the
press sit in at the United Nations. He was looking
around at some of the silliest things he had ever seen.
The man named Jarvis, whose history he knew, was
speaking to the U.N., and that by itself would have
been weird enough. But then all around Buff, people
were going loopy. First, everyone had started climbing
onto each other's shoulders while the little man swung
his watch and didn't say a word. Then the towers had
fallen, and various delegates were giving backrubs.
Japan was rubbing Mexico, Tanzania was rubbing
Turkey, and Israel, of all amazing wonders, was
rubbing New Zealand. And all the while the little man
up front didn't say a thing, he simply kept swinging
his watch.

"Is it possible that this little man who looks like
he sells carpet could hypnotize every delegate in the
United Nations simply with one or two fell swings of
his watch? No," thought Buff. Suddenly the Swiss
delegate jumped into the press area, and squeezed Buff
with all his Swiss might, and dashed off. "Yes,"
thought Buff. "It is possible."

Cleo was watching the United Nations monkeyshines with great interest. The little man up front hadn't done anything but swing his watch, but everyone else seemed to be having fun.

"Honey? What is that?" Buford asked.

"Oh, Daddy!" Cleo said. "You've gotten off the floor. Are you watching this?"

"Is that little guy up front supposed to be talking, or is he just doing a magic trick with his watch?"

"I don't know. He hasn't said anything so far. But I have a sinking suspicion about him."

"What's that?"

"I think the Tribulation is about to kick in."

"Why?"

"Daddy, I've had a different perspective on things since I got home. I converted. A truck driver prayed with me on my way here. The little guy with the watch feels evil to me. I think that's part of the package. When you convert, you can laugh at little guys with pocket watches. Are you interested in converting? I'd be happy to lead you in the prayer."

"I already converted," Buford said.

"I don't believe it! When?"

"Just now, on the floor with the cookie."

Haddie was enthralled. This man had ideas.

"Ninety-two percent of each of your country's arms will be destroyed. The other eight percent will be given to me personally. The keys to all the tanks and jeeps will be mailed to the following address. . ."

Haddie was so excited. Buff had promised to introduce her to this man, and she couldn't wait to have his baby. Such greatness must reproduce.

"In addition," the Antichrist continued, "only ten of you will be allowed to stay in the U.N. while the rest of you will function as slave states. Strawberry ice cream, strawberry flavoring, and even strawberries themselves are hereby banned on a global level. I am allergic to the beastly little things.

"Lastly for now, the headquarters of the United Nations is no longer in New York. The entire building, and even the delegates, shall in one week be moved to the city of Babylon. It is currently only a Kurdish trailer court, but I think if we move there, others will follow.

"I would once again like to thank you for choosing me as your Antichrist. I will do. . ." Haddie's phone rang.

"Hello?" Haddie said.

"Haddie. This is Buff. Do you still wanna warm the bed of the Antichrist?"

"Absolutely!"

"Did you see him on TV?"

"Yes. Isn't he gorgeous?"

"He looks like a small carpet salesman, but that's your call. If you want to meet him you can. He'll be at the Manhattan Comfort Inn for another week. Then apparently all the delegates are moving into mobile

homes in Northern Iraq. He'd like you to be there
tonight if you can. Haddie, he's an evil man."

"Yes, but so cute."

"Haddie, he asked me if you wear scarlet."

"I love scarlet, especially if he does."

"Haddie, the man laughed and said, 'The smoke
from her goes up forever.'"

"You know that I smoke."

"Haddie, he wants to make you the Whore of
Babylon."

"I'm no prude."

"He wants you to live in a trailer court with him."

"I'll talk to him about that one, but I'm sure that
it's a mere stepping stone. Thanks for all your help,
Buff. Now I've got to run and change into something
scarlet and head in to NYC. You'll see me on the
news."

"I'll write you in the news. 'Woman in Scarlet
Found Burning Forever' sounds about right."

———————

Now that both Buford and Cleo were Christians, they
decided to do two things, well, maybe three or perhaps four. The first was to track down Haddie and
witness to her. The second was to track down Buff
and witness to him. Buford had been feeling a real
burden for Buff, especially because he is one of the
main characters. The third was Cleo's idea. They
would stop by the church Eileen had attended to

commemorate both Little Bufie and Eileen. Then
they'd go bowling. The fourth would fit in anywhere.
They wanted to start singing gospel music.

They ended up doing things in somewhat of a
reverse order. They went bowling first and had a great
time. They played some pinball and ate some hot dogs
and had an all-around good morning, or afternoon.
Time seems to have lost itself in this story. Regardless,
they had their fun, and then they decided to stop by
the church before they tried to find Haddie and Buff.
They never sang gospel.

When they arrived at the church, an odd discovery
awaited. Actually, an odd discovery had awaited at the
church even before they had arrived, but it continued
to do so when they had. The odd discovery was Pastor
Bozeman.

The church doors had been open, and they had
walked right into the sanctuary and scene of Little
Bufie's exit. There were still a few patches of blood on
the cottage cheese ceilings, but the hole in the stained
glass had been repaired with cardboard and duct tape.

"Wow. I've never been in here before," Cleo said.

"I have, and I've never liked it before. I do now,"
Buford said. "It feels so holy. Now that I'm a Christian, I like holiness. Before it was just gold glitter in
the ceiling, but now it's angels' sparkle dust looking
over us, sent to twinkle-guide us through the Tribulation."

"Daddy," Cleo said, "that's beautiful. That's
something Mom would have said. Now that you are a

Christian, you can be my mom and my dad." And she
gave him a meaningful embrace. The meaningfulness
was mutual.

"Hey!" came a resounding voice. But something
was wrong. It sounded vaguely upside down.

"Hey!" it came again. "Who's out there?"

"We are!" responded Cleo. "Where are you?"

"I'm in my office! This is Pastor Bozeman speaking. To whom am I speaking?"

"Pastor Bozeman!" Buford and Cleo said at once.
"This is Buford Tin! Pastor Bozeman, why were you
left behind?"

"Come to my office, and we'll discuss it!"

"Where's your office?" Cleo asked.

"Just follow my voice! I'll yell as loud and as long
as I can, and you run after it!"

"Ha!" Buford said. "This sounds like fun, Cleo.
Okay Pastor Bozeman, YELL!" And the yell came.

"AAAAAAAAAAAAAAAAAAAAAAAAAAA!!!"
Pastor Bozeman said. Buford and Cleo found him
while he was still yelling.

———

Buff sat in room 103 of the Manhattan Comfort Inn.
The Antichrist sat across from him, chatting casually.
Buff was supposed to be grateful for this completely
exclusive opportunity with the new leader of
Antichristendom. But instead he simply sat and let the
Antichrist chatter while he thought of something else.

The something else he was thinking of happened to be himself. Buff was no egotist, at least not as much as he used to be. He was thinking about what had happened at the United Nations that afternoon. The little man had hypnotized the entire delegation present, as well as the press corp. Buff had checked the news after the speech, and all anyone could talk about was the new world leader. All the clips had been of someone wholly other than the little man in front of him. They had been of a tall, young, blonde, princely looking fellow. Nobody else had noticed the disparity. More than that, the little man now in front of him had not said a word during the entire forty-five minutes that he had stood in front of the delegates, and yet the crowd had all risen to their feet and applauded suddenly, but at the same time. The delegates had also acted like children, cartwheeling and dancing, and yet none of that was on the news. It was as if it hadn't been remembered.

Buff looked straight at the Antichrist, straight into his eyes. Nope, he was no tall, blonde prince. All this little man had done was waggle his watch a bit, and suddenly he was the most powerful man in the world. And the watch had worked over television. Viewers were raving about the speech and charisma of Old Nick Jarvis. Mobs were clamoring for one world government under his leadership, one currency, one religion, one language, one theme song.

"How is it that I am the only one who sees what he is? Is there something extra special in me that

makes me impossible to hypnotize?" The Antichrist
continued his mindless prattle about his plans, and
then Buff heard something that grabbed his attention.
Old Nick Jarvis had been in the middle of something
about global religion when he had mentioned the
'Christianity storehouse' and moved on to the subject
of church softball leagues.

"Did you say 'Christianity storehouse'?" Buff
asked.

"Haven't you been listening?"

"No. Not really. I've been preoccupied with
thoughts about your speech today. But you've got my
attention now."

"When did you expect your lady friend?" Old
Nick asked.

"Your lady friend you mean."

"No. I'm certain that I don't need a lady friend."

"But you told me to have her stop by tonight."

"Yes, but that was only because I thought you
would be here, and you wanted company."

"Antichrist Jarvis, you are the Antichrist, you
have made that clear. Yes? Well, where is your Whore
of Babylon? Who's going to believe that you're for real
if you don't have a whore?"

"Will Haddie be comfortable with that term?"

"Mr. Jarvis, Mr. Antichrist Jarvis, you really don't
need to worry about it. Haddie will take care of
herself. But I would like to know about this Christian
storage thing you referred to."

"Strictly off the record?"

"Yes."

"You are aware that according to popular works of apocalyptic fiction, if any information is prefaced with the phrase 'off the record,' then you can be sure that it won't be used?"

"I am aware of that, yes."

"Then here's your story. If you try to use it, you'll end up dead, like Durk Lynus."

"And Scott Henshaw."

"And Scott Henshaw, as well as a few hundred thousand Christians."

"What do you mean?"

"Well, if we are going to start at the beginning, I've been studying the Rapture for three decades. As I came to hate God, I realized that the Rapture typified everything that I hated about Christianity. It didn't affect anything in reality. Christians talked really big about being involved in politics and culture, but they simultaneously had no idea what that might mean. Everyone was always looking forward to the Rapture. My father and uncles were all pastors while they were young. And all of them attempted to construct something worth having, worth fighting and dying for. They attempted to construct a communal culture. But it was always shot down by the doctrine of the Rapture. No long-term plans are ever approved in Evangelical churches because nobody currently alive would get to see them. Besides, all the nice buildings just get left behind undefended against guys like me. So why build them?"

"Go on."

"Well, pretty early on I got the crazy idea that I might be able to prevent the Rapture. I immediately went to Brazil to study under the best international minds on the subject of spiritual density and magnetism.

"The idea was, and is, that if I can get all the Christians in one place for long enough, then I can prevent the Rapture through magnetism. I immediately began researching the technology needed and reading through the tough prophetic passages about me. I discovered certain theological truths that I will not mention because they would give everything away. But those are unimportant to you. What is important is that I did manage to fake the Rapture, and as a result, will be able to prevent it."

"You faked the Rapture? Where are the millions of people that disappeared?" Buff was genuinely curious, though he didn't know whether to believe this man or simply consider him insane.

"They have all been transported to an enormous, though highly secure, theme park that I created for the purpose."

"They're all naked, minus fillings and appendixes?"

"I'm afraid so. There are a few things that were unanticipated, though I am grateful that the cotton went with them. They have plenty of clothing and won't be terribly cold."

"They are in some place cold?"

"As I told you, they are in a highly secure theme park. All the rides are free. The theme park is called New Babylon, and all the rides relate to exile. It is actually situated in the far northern territories of Canadia."

"Canada?"

"Canadia is its new name."

Buff was astonished by all this. He found himself believing the little man.

"But why are you telling me all this? Why share your Rapture secret with me?" Buff asked. The little man named Jarvis laughed.

"Because it is a fun story to tell, and I need not worry about you talking. For all the talk of 'off the record,' you could still run to press with this in the morning."

"Except my boss Steve loves you."

"You'll be dead by the end of the night, so it's irrelevant," said the Antichrist, and he picked his teeth with his thumbnail.

There was a knock on the door. Both Old Nick Jarvis and Buff ignored it. There was a deep spiritual conflict flickering and flashing between their eyes. Buff's eyes were blue, Jarvis's green.

"How am I going to die?" Buff said. There was a knock at the door.

"You are going to die a violent death." Jarvis continued picking his teeth. He had eaten corn-on-the-cob for dinner and had been struggling with the remains ever since.

"What sort of violence?" Buff said.

"My sort. I have killed before."

"No, you haven't. You don't have the look of a killer," said Buff. There was a knock on the door.

"Yes, I have. I don't mind spilling blood, and I most certainly have the look. My eye has a steely hate and despair that means that I fear no man. I am ready at any point during the day to kill if need be. I'll even hit and run. I've done it before."

"Hello?" came Haddie's muffled voice through the door. "Is this the Antichrist's room? Is anyone there?"

"Yes!" both men yelled.

"Hold on a second!" Jarvis added. He looked at Buff. Buff looked at him. He looked Buff up and down. "I am going to get the door," Jarvis said. "You will wait right here, Mr. Williamson." He waved his hand in front of his face in Eastern-mystic fashion. Then he rose from his seat and walked to the door, watching Buff all the while. When he reached the door, he turned quickly to let Haddie in.

Buff took off his shoe and leapt to his feet in one swift motion.

"Your Jedi mind tricks don't work on me, Jarvis!" he shrieked. He brought the shoe down hard onto the top of the surprised man's little head and burst out the door into the hall, bowling Haddie over just outside. He sprinted off down the hall, clopping along with one shoe, the Antichrist hot on his heels.

Both men regretted the fact that the Antichrist's suite had been on the first floor. It would have been rather exciting to leap downstairs, crashing into walls and knocking people over. But the room was on the first floor, so Buff was in the lobby before he knew it and immediately afterward was running through the parking lot. He jumped two juniper bushes in a single, slow motion leap, leading with his socked foot and then hit the sidewalk on the other side in full speed. His legs were burning with desire to just keep running; he had a techno sound track in his head, and he felt that no man alive could stick to his pace. But he wasn't being chased by just any man.

The Antichrist had been surprised at first. His feelings had been more injured by the shoe than his head. How had his magic not affected Buff? Regardless of the answer, he wasn't about to let him get away. He had hopped over Haddie's prostrate form immediately and sped after Buff. As Buff leapt the junipers, he had already been closing the gap. He had always been the best at the relay races in Sunday school and still maintained the same confidence and training that he had in those days of his youth.

As both men tore down the sidewalk through Manhattan, Jarvis opened conversation.

"Buff! Ha, Ha, Ha! Buff!" he said. "You can't outrun me. I'm Old Nick Jarvis!"

"Pipsqueak!" Buff said. And he shot an unmentionable obscene gesture over his shoulder. He immediately wished that he hadn't. The Antichrist scooped an old canning jar out of a trash can and let fly at Buff's speeding back. It hit Buff in the neck, and he went down hard. Buff had tried to keep his feet under himself, but he slowly dove with palms extended to the sidewalk, his soundtrack slowing down as he ducked his head to try and somersault his way out of it. He hit his head on the concrete and was down, flat and bleeding. The Antichrist was on his back immediately. He felt hands grip his head in preparation to snap his neck.

"Wait! Hold on a second! Jarvis wait! Hold on! Can I say something?" Buff said.

"What?" Jarvis said, but he didn't loosen his grip.

"Ow, Ow, Ow!" Buff said. "At least let go and let me say something." Jarvis let go of his head, but his knee was pressed firmly into his *right behind*.

"Okay!" Buff said. "I really don't think we should be doing this. We might get in trouble."

"Why?" Jarvis said.

"Well, this is an Evangelical novel. I know you're the villain, and I'm a good guy, but we shouldn't be fighting, we should be having an Evangelical conversation."

"We already did that."

"I know, but would anything like this actually happen in the real book? There wasn't any action. We should be dialoguing."

"There were a couple of places with action in the real book. What about the car bomb? Or the wrestling match you had in the hotel? Or the shooting in the U.N.?"

"But that's it, right? There was no actual conflict

between the forces of good and evil, and yet here we are, conflicting."

"You're right," Jarvis said. "I'm the Antichrist. If we allow any direct conflict between the good characters and the bad, then we have undermined the length of our series. Hmmm, what do you think. . ."

At this point the Antichrist was sufficiently distracted for Buff to make his move. He writhed quickly onto his back, knocking the Antichrist to his side. Then Buff bit him. He bit his eyebrow, and he bit it hard and long.

"Ow!" the Antichrist yelled. "You hypocritical little—"

"Careful," Buff said. "No obscenities!" And he was on his feet and running.

The Antichrist's head was wounded, but he was on his feet as well. Buff had left the sidewalk and was heading for a storefront. It appeared to be a dealer of knick knacks. Buff barreled inside just ahead of the Antichrist. Glancing around, he realized what it was. He stopped and turned to face his evil opponent.

"Old Nick! You can do no harm to me here! Your power is nothing. Your will is jelly, and your strength cookie dough! Turn and depart, oh demon of the night! We are in a *Christian* bookstore." Jarvis looked around him and laughed.

"Ha!" he said. "Ha! So we are. And a fitting place for you to die, surrounded by the wreckage of a weak culture. Christianity's weakness is no threat to me. In it lies my strength!" And he began walking toward

Buff. Buff was unnerved. Grabbing at some small, cute, ceramic representations of children apostles, he pelted them at the Antichrist. They bounced off or shattered but did no hurt to the man.

Jarvis closed his eyes and stood, completely disregarding the missiles. The clerk who had been stocking the Veggie Tale shelves peered out to see what the ruckus was. When he saw, he didn't say anything. He would have liked to, but such surroundings breed fear and weakness. He desperately wished he could be as brave as King David-the-cucumber and kick the evil-looking carpet fellow out, but instead he just sat down on the floor and cried, not quite to sleep, but almost.

"Ha!" Jarvis said. "Surrender to your fate now Cameroon Williamson."

"No!" Buff said and he leapt onto the counter and pulled a Thomas Kinkaid painting off the wall. It was framed, behind glass, and would pack a punch. Jarvis approached. Buff brought it down onto the Antichrist's head. The glass shattered, the frame broke, the print wrinkled, but the painting lit up.

"Ooh, neat," said Buff. Jarvis kept laughing. He jumped onto the counter as well. Buff was frozen, looking at the glowing painting in his hands. Now simply chuckling to himself, Jarvis scooped up the cash register and smacked Buff with it. Buff fell and lay stricken among the shards of Precious Moments figurines that he had thrown, a glowing print clutched to his chest.

———————

Cleo and Buford entered Pastor Bozeman's office cautiously. It was a large office and packed with paperbacks. In the center of the room sat a simple oak veneer desk and one of those lamps trying so hard to be something with its little green glass shade. Above the desk on the ceiling, next to the ceiling fan, sat a large man with a book. He was of an African complexion and was wearing a suit big enough for his body.

"Hello, Buford. Hello, Cleo. I know you both through the prayers of Eileen. She would come into the church and kneel at the altar and pray. I would sneak quietly up behind her to find out what she was praying for. She was praying for you two."

"Why are you on the ceiling?" Cleo asked.

"Why do you think?"

"I have no idea."

"Really? Buford, can you do better than your daughter?"

"You were Raptured in the same way as my wife and son, only they went out windows. Why have you stayed? It's been at least a week now. Have you been on this ceiling the whole time? How do you go to the bathroom?"

"There's a bathroom attached to this office. I just crawl in there."

"Why don't you walk?" Cleo asked. Pastor Bozeman looked confused.

"You know, this whole week I haven't tried to stand on the ceiling once." Slowly he clambered onto all fours and then stood up, or down. His face was now even with Cleo's shoulders and reached Buford's lower ribs.

"Doesn't the blood rush to your head?" Buford asked.

"Oh no, my blood is being sucked up as well as my body. It doesn't drain down. If I were to stand on the floor with you, chained down, all the blood would rush to my head."

"Is it uncomfortable having your suit hang around your ears that way, or do you get used to it?" Cleo asked.

"I'm used to it already. But what brings you two here? I can only assume that you have come to commemorate the loss of two such lovely family members." Pastor Bozeman's voice was soothing. Both Buford and Cleo nodded.

"Do you think that they are in Heaven?" Pastor Bozeman asked.

"Yes," Buford said.

"Of course," Cleo said.

"They aren't," the upside-down pastor looked toward the ceiling and Buford's chin as if delivering bad news. He was. "They, and every other Christian who isn't still sitting on his ceiling or hanging onto a tree branch, have been sucked off to a theme park in the far Northern reaches of Canada. They may or may not be alive, but they have not been Raptured. They have been abducted in an attempt to prevent the Rapture, but I'm afraid that isn't the primary goal of our enemy. His primary goal is to prevent the Tribulation, and if he does that, he will have brought our entire dispensation to its knees, and kicked it in the teeth, a thing we can't allow to happen.

Buford and Cleo both sat down quietly. This man spoke truth. They could feel it in their freshly minted Evangelical bones. Eileen and Bufie were in Canada.

"Eileen always got sick at theme parks," Buford said.

"This one will be no different. It's called New Babylon. I'm afraid there's no hope for the motion sick."

"But what will we do?" Cleo said. Her little pouty lip was trembling as she asked.

"Whatever I tell you to. I have been studying and preparing for this day for a long time. I am ready to match my wits with the Antichrist! I am strong and I roar like the lion of Judah!" And with that the big man threw his hands down toward the floor, fists clenched. His eyes were closed and rage and love filled his mighty black face. He roared. Buford and Cleo jumped back in awe.

"Truly," thought Buford, "this is a prophet!" The roaring stopped, but Pastor Bozeman kept his fists toward the floor and his eyes closed. His suit hung around his ears and more. When he was finished he looked at both of them.

"I have had a vision," he said. "We must pray for

Buff Williamson. He is in great peril. His life is in danger, though his soul is safe."

"Buff Williamson has converted?" Cleo asked.

"Yes," said Pastor Bozeman, "though he does not know it yet. You must find him and bring him here as soon as possible."

"He was on my flight when the Rapture hit. I think Haddie was going to keep in touch with him."

"Call her and find out," Bozeman said. "But before you do, I think we all need a hug." They hugged, two on the floor hugging one on the ceiling.

"This lion needs a lioness," Pastor Bozeman whispered in Cleo's ear.

Haddie's cell phone was ringing.

"How embarrassing," thought Buff. His hands were tied in the small of his back. His feet were tied as well, but not in the small of his back. He couldn't believe the little Antichrist had caught up to him and worked him over.

"Hello," Haddie said into the phone. She was looking classy in a scarlet evening dress. The Antichrist was in the bathroom. It was his big chance. He wriggled and squirmed, but the knots held firm.

"Yeah, he's right here, but he can't talk right now. Can I give him a message?" Buff kept squirming. "You want me to tell him that he's in grave danger and to give you a call when he gets out of it. OK. Easy enough. I'll do that. No, I have your number, so I can give it to him. What was that? You want me to come to dinner?"

Buff was frantic now. He knew the Antichrist couldn't be in the john much longer. A sweat of panic broke out on his forehead; he knew he was going to die.

Suddenly, a serenity came upon Buff, a peacefulness that he had only known once. It was the realization that as bad as things were, it was only a story.

"It's only a story," he told himself.

"It's only a story," he told himself.

"It's only a story," he told himself.

"How sweet!" Haddie said. Suddenly, Buff's knots loosened. It was only a story! Relief coursed through his veins as he leapt to his feet. Grabbing Haddie, he kissed her.

"It's only a story!" he shouted. Flinging open the bathroom door, he said his farewells to the Antichrist.

"Best of luck in the rest of the series!" he hollered at the embarrassed man on the john. He hesitated, thinking perhaps a simple farewell wasn't enough. He ran into the bathroom, kicked the horrified little man off the toilet, and fled using his two legs.

FIVE:
TRIBULATION TEAM

BUFF had called Haddie's cell phone from the first pay
phone he found.

"What was the message for me?" he asked.

"Oh, I'm sorry. I should have given that to you.
Buford Tin wanted you to call him as soon as you
escaped. I have his number right here."

Thirty minutes later Buff was on a bus to Chicago.
The Antichrist had immediately called Buff's boss and
had him fired. When Buff had called in to check his
voicemail, he had a message telling him not to bother
coming in ever again. Buff was sad. But he still had his
youthful vigor, so he pressed on.

He had called Buford Tin and been invited to

come stay with them for a while. Apparently Buford
knew more about Buff's internal struggle than Buff
did. Of course character development and recognition
is notoriously lax in this genre. Buford made a few
comments about being "saved" that Buff didn't quite
follow. Of course now that he was on a bus to Chicago, he had a lot of time to think through where he
stood spiritually. Things had been puzzling him since
the U.N. meeting where sanity had come unhinged.
Why had the Antichrist had no effect on him? Buford
had acted like he knew the answer. He talked to Buff
as if salvation had protected him. But had it?

It was somewhere in Indiana that it came back to
him. He'd been so busy that he'd forgotten all about
it. Right before the Jarvis speech, Buff had dashed into
the restroom. It was in the bathroom that he had given
himself over to God. He had even sat and wept on the
floor under the conviction of his sins. So he had been
saved! What a close shave! If he hadn't prayed the
prayer just then, he would probably be as in love with
Jarvis as Haddie, though in a different way.

There was a woman sitting next to Buff who
looked like she needed a friend.

"Excuse me ma'am," Buff said, "I'm Buff
Williamson, and I have many awards and achieve-
ments in my past. But I think you should know that I
esteem you above all of them. Do you feel loved and
accepted?" The woman looked back at him respond-
ing with blank silence. Buff's conversion memory had
stirred a great goodness in his soul.

"Your silence only tells me of your pain," Buff said. "I hope you realize that I don't ever normally do this type of thing, but I think you need a hug. If it would make it easier, you could pretend that I'm the one who needs a hug, and you're the one giving. That might be easier on your pride, and you'd still get hugged." There was still no response, so Buff decided to rein in his new-found religious exuberance. If the lady didn't want a hug, she didn't have to have one.

"Just know that I'm always here," he said, "if you ever need one." He hadn't talked to anybody else for the rest of the drive. He just gazed out the window and thought over all that had happened in the last few days. There wasn't much, so he gave up on that and began naming the cows grazing by the side of the road. Time passed in the same way it had in the rest of this story, at irregular intervals.

Buff was unsure of his future. He didn't have a job. That's what made him unsure. He did know a little something about his future. He had called the Tins to tell them when he would be getting in to the bus station and had been told that Cleo would be picking him up.

"I hope you don't mind if I'm not there to pick you up," Buford had said. "I'll be in a meeting with Pastor Bozeman. I could get out of it, but Cleo was hoping to spend some time with you. She's seen your picture you know."

"No, I didn't know. Which picture?"

"Oh, just one she found online. She's a very pretty girl you know."

"I did know that. You can stop this plugging your daughter business. You know that I'm going to fall for her anyway. Oh, I'm sorry. That was my old pre-Christian crankiness coming out. Tell me about your daughter, Mr. Tin." And so it had gone. Buford had gone on for quite some time about the marvels of his daughter Cleo, and Buff had listened politely until he suddenly realized that he was listening intently.

Cleo was getting quite the buildup. Buff hoped that she lived up to it. Cleo did not know about the buildup. She still doesn't, so don't tell her.

Haddie sat on the edge of the bed in room 103. There was a big decision ahead of her. Old Nick Jarvis was leaving for Babylon and wanted her to come with him and wear scarlet. But there was a slight doubt in her mind. When Buff had been trussed up by Old Nick, she had watched cheerfully, because the man doing the trussing was the same gorgeous man she had fallen for. But she had begun to have her suspicions about the true nature of her lover.

Buff had kicked him off the toilet. That was unflattering in the first place, a bit of an embarrassment for a man of power and authority. Haddie had not gone in to help. It seemed only natural that her Old Nick could handle the situation on his own. But then he had called for her help. His pants had twisted funny when he tried to dodge the kick, and the kick

itself had lodged him pretty sturdily between the little
bathtub and the john. He was on his side, legs and
arms stuck, hollering for help.

Even this would not have bothered Haddie, she
was so sold on Jarvis. What bothered her was that the
little man stuck between the toilet and the tub was not
the same man that she had seen on TV and fallen in
love with. It was a little man who looked as if he sold
used carpets and mattresses. After she had helped him
up and turned her back, her beautiful lover had
returned, but she remained unsettled.

Now that he wanted her to come to Babylon, she
had to decide whether or not it mattered to her if she
loved an illusion or an actuality. For all the build up, it
didn't take her long to decide. She liked wearing
scarlet and would make a home in Babylon.

Cleo stood nervously waiting for the bus to unload.
She knew exactly what Buff looked like and was eager
to see him smile and walk toward her. When Buff
stepped off the bus, he hadn't shaved and was carrying
his jacket and a small leather case in one hand while
the other hand ran through his hair. His shirt was
unbuttoned just enough to tastefully display the chest
and its foliage. It was all on purpose. He knew he
looked good. Cleo wasn't so confident. She had
snacked in the car out of nervousness and then, in an
attempt to remove the evidence, had brushed her teeth
without water in the parking lot.

Buff was stunned when he saw her. He had loved her name from the first time he had heard it, and it fit her, so beautiful and elegant. She looked like a long e, long o progression.

"You must be Cleo," Buff said. "The sunshine fades in your presence."

"And you are Buff. I've seen your picture and read your articles, but I have to say that I like your ghost-writing best." Buff smiled and laughed at such beauty's admiration. Looking back at her face he noticed that she had some junk in the corners of her mouth.

"Do you mind?" he asked and stuck his thumb out. She held up her chin prettily. Buff swiped the left corner first and then realized that he had painted himself in a corner. Of course she would expect him to eat it. If he wiped it off his thumb onto something, then he was tacky and grossed out by her gunk. He couldn't afford to look like either, so the little gob went into his smiling mouth.

"Oh, how romantic!" she said and showed him the other side. "Anything over here?" she asked. He had been planning on ignoring the second gob, but his hand had been dealt. So, the other corner got swiped an eaten as well. This time there was a little twitch of the face that made Cleo curious.

"What was it?" she asked.

"Toothpaste."

"Oh sick."

"Not as bad as the first one."

"Which was?"

"Cheese." By the time they reached Hoping to Endtimes Church, the toothpaste taste was gone and the Buff/Cleo relationship was well under way, peppered with lots of corny age jokes and forced laughter.

———————

Buford Tin sat across the desk from Pastor Bozeman. Pastor was sitting cross-legged just above his desk. Scattered around on the ceiling there were a few pillows stapled. The Pastor was sitting on one now.

"Are you sure they are going to come in as soon as they get here?" Pastor Bozeman asked.

"Positive," said Buford, and as he spoke the door swung open and Cleo and Buff entered.

"Buff! Good to see you again," said Buford. "This is Pastor Bozeman. He's our leader. Cleo and I are researchers, and we also. . . .Actually, perhaps it would be better if Pastor Bozeman explained the whole situation before we got into role explanations. Pastor?"

"Very nice to meet you Buff," said Pastor Bozeman.

"You as well," Buff replied.

"I like your hair."

"Thanks."

"Do you have it done like that, or is it just that way?"

"Both. The curls are natural, but I like to accentuate sometimes."

"That's exactly my philosophy. Anyway, we ought to get down to business. To begin, perhaps I had better explain this past Rapture, or at least, how I was able to anticipate it.

"I have long studied endtimes and had a very standard view of the Rapture. It was coming soon, and before the Tribulation. I preached this regularly, as did every other pastor I know. But it was about a year ago when something in the Old Testament genealogies jumped out at me. I won't give you the passage because it doesn't make sense without the decoder ring anyway. But, it was a numerical prophecy and as obvious as two plus twelve once the equation had been worked out."

At this point, to Buff's further amazement, the big man stood up and began pacing the ceiling as he talked. His suit coat slipped too far over his face, so he shook it off onto the floor and continued pacing. His red tie was pinned in the middle and had folded over the point.

"The prophecy that I had discovered and my peers would not believe was the prophecy of this past pseudo-Rapture. The prophecy spoke of a man raising himself up as a false Antichrist and attacking the Rapture itself. He would Rapture the Christians to his own kingdom so that he could prevent them from Rapturing when the true time came. This may all seem strange, but it gets more complicated. If the real Rapture is thwarted, then there will be no Tribulation, and without the Tribulation, we have completely lost our dispensation. All of our doctrines will be replaced, and we will be living in an entirely new system. And that system will be no fun at all!

"The dispensation that our false Antichrist could usher in is lengthy. Under its rule, Christians would be forced to look thousands of years ahead to the Second Coming. We would be forced to build a culture that would last gloriously in Christ until He came. We would no longer have any short-term hope. Everything would become slow and arduous. We would be under a system of covenants, and Christ would not return until the Great Commission had been fulfilled.

"Even though you three are still fresh in the faith, you can see what a tragedy this shift would be. It would bring back all the medieval church's obsessions with the earth and physical labor. It would remove the hard fought and won principles that piety exists in the immaterial being of a person and cannot find its home in actions but must reside in thoughts.

"I could go on. The choice is clear. Christians are being held hostage, but through them the Rapture itself becomes threatened, and through it, the Tribulation."

"Sorry to interrupt," said Cleo. "What would happen to all the souls that would have converted through the Evangelical purgatory of the Tribulation but don't know they need to convert because the Church is building instead of preaching?"

"That's a good question. Those souls would be lost. But we now get to the crux of this meeting and why we have dragged Buff here?"

"We are forming a Tribulation Team."

"And what is our mission?" Buff asked.

"To rescue the Tribulation from those who are holding it hostage, and in doing so, rescuing dispensationalism from certain doom. We will fight the false Antichrist at every step of the way. We will do battle with him for more than the body of Moses. Our treasure is more precious than Moses because he was flesh, and we pursue the immaterial truths of a systematic. We will have assigned tasks, but for now it is good enough to know that we are a team."

"Can you come with us when we go on missions?" Buff asked.

"Buford and I were talking about that before you came in. He is making a leash that will keep me from being sucked off to the theme park whenever we're outside or I am disinclined to use the ceiling. Anymore questions?"

"I think we need a cheer," said Cleo.

"Okay! Everybody in. Circle up!" Pastor Bozeman stuck one fist toward the floor while he yelled. The others gathered around his fist, placing their hands on it.

"Like lions now," said Pastor Bozeman. "1. . . 2. . . 3. . ." and then with one collective, powerful, almost to the point of a cookie voice, they all shouted,

"TEAM!"

The sanctuary shook. Gold glitter fell. The book ended in a moment of triumph.

After the book ended, they fell into each other's arms, relieved that it was over.

"This is horrible! How could anyone possibly save dispensationalism, especially us?" Buff wept. While the tears flowed, they pulled Pastor Bozeman off of the ceiling and sat on him to keep him down. And there, in a huddled pile on the big man's chest, they cried themselves to sleep.

The Upturned Table Parody Series

The "upturned table" in our series name points back to Christ's anger with the merchants in the temple. Our parody series isn't as concerned with money in the Temple as it is with what modern Evangelicals spend on abject silliness. Now you can't say that sort of thing or publish parodies without someone pointing out that you're no genius yourself. And we don't claim to be. First, we see our parodies as sermons—to ourselves before anyone else. For we too are responsible for the lame state of popular Evangelicalism today, even those of us who are from more classical Protestant backgrounds. We, too, exhibit some of the targets of our own barbs. Second, we also don't claim to sit aloof, all clean and wise, looking down on others' silliness. We are a part of the Evangelical community ourselves. These are our brothers who write these things; they represent us too. We have no doubts about their sincerity and good-hearted goals and wonderful characters, but we all must do light-years better.

The first response from many who love the books we aim to skewer is to be "wounded" and "offended," but that is the tiresome refuge of every little god who thinks blasphemy restrictions apply to him (oooh, notice the evil gender violation there). We all need to grow up and take the heat. But what about all those for whom these "precious" books have meant so much? One answer is that medieval folks could say the same thing about their relics. Relics made people feel warm and fuzzy too, but they were evidence of sickness.

Christian reality is a rich and fascinating blend of truth, beauty, and goodness. It is an exuberant love of life and light and celebration. Even with some of the glorious heights of Christian culture reached in prior eras, the Church still hasn't truly begun to plumb the magnificence of the Triune God. We're only scratching the surface, all the while non-Christian visions are perennially addicted to death. In order to mature, Evangelicals need to move beyond the bumper sticker shallowness of the past four decades and long for true wisdom. Parodying our silliness is one small nudge in that direction. *To whom much is given, much is expected.*

Be sure to visit the Canon Press web site
for our other books:

www.canonpress.org
1–800–488–2034

including such titles such as:

• *Angels in the Architecture: A Protestant Vision
for Middle Earth* by Douglas Jones and Douglas
Wilson (Canon Press)
• *Plowing in Hope: Toward a Biblical Theology of
Culture* by David Bruce Hegeman (Canon Press)
• *Last Days Madness: Obsession of the Modern
Church* by Gary DeMar (American Vision)
• *Postmillennialism: An Eschatology of Hope* by
Keith A. Mathison (Presbyterian & Reformed Publ.)
• *A House for My Name: A Survey of the Old
Testament* by Peter J. Leithart (Canon Press)
• *The Roar on the Other Side: A Guide for
Student Poets* by Suzanne U. Clark (Canon Press)
• *Reforming Marriage* by Douglas Wilson (Canon
Press)
• *Future Men: Raising Boys* by Douglas Wilson
(Canon Press)
. . . and more.

See *Credenda/Agenda* magazine too:
www.credenda.org